Ruby smiled at Chuck. "It might be fun to ride together for a while. But if you guys find I'm slowing you down you need to go on ahead and not worry about Lancelot and me."

"You'll probably do better than me," Chuck said with a shrug.

"We'll stay together if it works for us then," Jeff said. "If it's holding anyone back, then it's every man for himself. Or woman."

Ruby grinned. "Got it. Do you want me to start out slower— just trot along?"

"No need," Jeff said. "We'll catch up. Right, Chuck?"

"Sure." Chuck wondered if he'd just agreed to an alliance that would cost him Ruby's attentions as well as a chance to lead the pack for a while. Once Jeff caught up to him and Ruby, there would be no question of who the ultimate winner would be. And as far as Ruby's heart was concerned. . .he eyed her as she chatted with Jeff. Her smile for the champ was as bright as the one she'd bestowed on Chuck earlier.

SUSAN PAGE DAVIS and her husband, Jim, have been married thirty-three years and have six children, ages fourteen to thirty-one, and five grandchildren. They live in Maine, where they are active in an independent Baptist church. Susan is a homeschooling mother and writes historical romance, mystery, and suspense novels. Visit her Web site at: www.susanpagedavis.com.

Books by Susan Page Davis

HEARTSONG PRESENTS
HP607—Protecting Amy
HP692—The Oregon Escort
HP708—The Prisoner's Wife
HP719—Weaving a Future
HP727—Wyoming Hoofbeats
HP739—The Castaway's Bride
HP756—The Lumberjack's Lady
HP800—Return to Love
HP811—A New Joy
HP827—Abiding Peace

Trail to Justice

Susan Page Davis

Heartsong Presents

To Vickie McDonough and Diana Brandmeyer. Working with you two on this series was a joy. I wish you great success in your writing careers and joy in the Lord.

Acknowledgment:
Thank you, Carl Wiggin, for advice on the airplane-related sections of this book. Any mistakes are totally my fault.

A note from the Author:
I love to hear from my readers! You may correspond with me by writing:

Susan Page Davis
Author Relations
PO Box 721
Uhrichsville, OH 44683

ISBN 978-1-60260-437-7

TRAIL TO JUSTICE

Our mission is to publish and distribute inspirational products offering exceptional value and biblical encouragement to the masses.

PRINTED IN THE U.S.A.

one

Ruby Dale let her palomino gelding, Lancelot, canter across the prairie toward home. They'd had a good workout—twenty miles plus—but Lancelot was still ready to go. In two weeks he'd demonstrate his mettle at the Wyoming 100 competitive trail ride, but she didn't need that proof to know he was at the peak of condition. Both were more than ready for the hundred-mile ride.

This was what she loved—getting out away from the claustrophobic atmosphere at home and her stressful job at the police station, alone with her horse. The burnished gold palomino had given her many hours of comfort in the last few years. If only Julie were riding beside her.

She was about to pull Lancelot down to a walk to cool him off when he missed his footing. He stumbled, lurching to the side. Ruby flew forward onto his neck, clutching desperately at his mane. She slid down his shoulder but tried to push herself upright as the horse recovered and found his footing again. Too late. Her center of gravity had shifted too far. She wouldn't be able to get back up into the saddle.

"Whoa, boy!" she called as she slipped down his side. For a moment she hung helpless, clinging to his mane. Her foot inched over the saddle. This was always the worst instant of a fall, not knowing how you'd land. She tucked her head and pushed off, falling hard on her left shoulder, and rolled quickly away from the horse's hooves. For a long moment she lay panting in the dry grass assessing her pains. Nothing major. Good thing, or her parents would have fits and forbid her to ride alone, even though she was twenty-four and well into adulthood.

Slowly she raised her head. Lancelot had halted and stood shivering a few yards away. She rose stiffly and stretched out her limbs. Nothing broken, but she'd have some colorful bruises by morning. She hobbled to the palomino's side and stroked his withers. "Are you all right?"

She grasped his reins and urged him to walk forward. Lancelot gave a decided hop to avoid putting weight on his off front hoof. Ruby ducked under his neck to his right side.

"Let me look, fella." She bent to lift his front foot, and Lancelot raised it for her. "Oh, man. Lost a shoe." She surveyed the chipped horn around the edge of his hoof. "I was going to have the blacksmith come next week, but I guess we need to get him over here sooner." She sighed. "I hope you're all right." She unbuttoned the pocket on her denim shirt and pulled out her cell phone. Her father insisted she always carry it on her long rides, and though she sometimes felt a bit smothered, this time she was grateful.

"Hey, Dad? It's me. Lancelot threw a shoe."

"What? Are you okay?"

"Yeah, I'm fine. I don't think he's hurt either, but I'm going to walk him home. We're only about a mile out."

"Let me come get you."

"No, really. We're okay. We'll just take our time." She glanced down at the palomino's feet. He was holding his right front foot off the ground.

"Where are you?" her father asked. "I can hitch up the trailer and come after you."

"Well. . .okay. Maybe that would be best. We're near the Danbridge Road." She looked around. "Maybe a half mile past Simpsons'."

"Okay, I'll be there in ten minutes."

"Thanks. We'll get up to the edge of the road." She put the

phone away and patted Lancelot's neck. "Okay, boy. Let's go."

She led him slowly through the grass, and Lancelot kept pace with only a slight limp. Still, it was enough to worry her. Would it keep him from entering the ride two weeks from today? She opened her phone again and keyed in the number for the veterinary clinic. Dr. John Hogan, the senior doctor in the practice, answered.

"Hi, Dr. Hogan. This is Ruby Dale. My horse threw a shoe, and I wondered if you or Dr. Sullivan could look at him. We're training for a competitive ride, and I don't want to keep exercising him if it's going to hurt him."

"Sure, Ruby. Let's see. Chuck is off today, but I'll give him a buzz and see if he's able to stop by. If he can't, I'll come over in about an hour. Is that all right?"

"It's perfect. Thank you."

She pocketed the phone and resumed the walk up to the roadbed. By the time she and Lancelot climbed up the grassy bank, a cloud of dust in the distance told her that her father was on his way.

&

The veterinarian's pickup rolled into the driveway a half hour later. Ruby hurried out to meet him, surprised after what Dr. Hogan had told her it was Dr. Chuck Sullivan responding. Not only that, but his truck was pulling a horse trailer. Lancelot seemed to have recovered his animation, and he trotted back and forth in his paddock and whinnied. An answering neigh erupted from the trailer.

"Hi! Thanks for coming on a Saturday," Ruby called as Chuck got out of the truck. She'd managed to skirt the issue of her own fall, and her parents were satisfied she was all right. If they'd thought she was injured, Mom and Dad would be out there watching her like a couple of hypervigilant hawks.

"No problem," Chuck said. "This actually worked out well

for me. I was just on my way home from a long ride. I took Rascal up to the hills this morning."

Ruby glanced toward the trailer. "Rascal is your horse? I didn't know you had one."

Chuck grinned, clearly pleased with his mount. "Yeah, I got him last spring. He's an Appaloosa. I've been riding him a lot, and we're starting to get comfortable with each other. Want to see him?"

"Sure." Ruby followed him to the rear of the trailer.

Chuck lowered the back door that made a loading ramp. The horse's well-muscled haunches were a snowy white, flecked with dark spots in a flamboyant blanket pattern. Chuck climbed the ramp into the empty side of the trailer, and Ruby followed. Her pulse accelerated as the horse whinnied again and tossed his head.

"Easy now." Chuck stroked the gelding's cheek.

"He's beautiful." Ruby reached out to pat the warm, dark withers. "How old?"

"Seven."

"Perfect."

"Yeah," Chuck said. "I figure he's the prime age for endurance riding."

"You're getting into distance riding?" Ruby looked up eagerly into his blue eyes.

"I sure am. You know I've volunteered for a couple of years at the Wyoming 100, and I've been jealous of the riders. I decided to let someone else man the checkpoint this year and compete myself."

"That's great." More than great, Ruby thought. "I'm riding, too."

"Terrific. Lancelot and Rascal will get to know each other." Chuck gave Rascal a soft slap on the neck and turned away.

Ruby swallowed hard and looked out toward the paddock.

"That is, I'm riding if Lancelot's foot is okay."

"We'd better take a look. Dr. Hogan said you had a little mishap?"

She nodded. "Yeah, we were loping across a field, and Lancelot threw a shoe and stumbled. He limped a little at first, but now that he's had a short rest he's putting weight on it again. I probably got you out here for nothing."

"Let's hope you're right."

Ruby hated to end the moment of camaraderie, but she edged over to the ramp and walked down it. Chuck stopped at his truck to retrieve his on-the-road medical case. "Okay, do you want to hold him while I examine him?"

"I'll put him in the cross ties." Ruby went to the paddock fence where Lancelot waited eagerly, his muzzle over the top of the gate. She grabbed his halter and swung the gate open with her other hand. The palomino walked meekly beside her into the barn and let her hitch him in the alley between the stalls, with a rope clipped to the rings on each side of his halter.

"Looking good so far. I can't even tell which leg."

"Oh, it's the right front."

Chuck ran a hand down Lancelot's off foreleg and lifted his hoof. "I always know I'll see a healthy horse when I come here, Ruby."

"Thank you." She stood by Lancelot's head and scratched beneath his forelock.

"How's your training for the ride going?" Chuck asked.

"Good until today. We've been doing ten miles or so mornings and one longer ride on the weekends." Calm down, she told herself. She sounded like an eager twelve-year-old. She shrugged with a little laugh. "I'm starting to believe we'll be able to finish."

"Sure you will."

"I don't know," she said. "We did two fifty-milers last year, but this will be our first one-hundred."

"Well, it's my first long ride, too. But the woman who owned Rascal had been training him for a while before I bought him, and I think he's ready." Chuck turned to his medical case and pulled out a file. "I don't feel any swelling or hot spots on his leg. I'm going to smooth this hoof up a little so he doesn't chip it any worse before the blacksmith comes."

"Thanks," Ruby said. "Dad called him, and he said he'll come Monday. I won't ride Lancelot tomorrow."

"That's wise." Chuck bent over the horse's hoof again. "Still working at the police station?"

"Yes."

"How's that going?"

"I love it," Ruby said, "but I've been putting in a lot of hours lately. They need to hire one more dispatcher to fill out the schedule."

"Cutting into your riding time?"

She nodded. "Some. I've had to pull a few double shifts lately while the officers were out chasing cocaine dealers. That doesn't happen often, though."

"I hope not. I imagine they want their dispatchers to stay alert."

She'd liked Chuck since she'd first met him three years ago. Okay, more than liked him. But she'd tried not to make it too obvious. Perhaps as a result she'd never had a chance to get to know him well. The older veterinarian, Dr. Hogan, had brought Chuck on board in his practice to handle the large animal part of the business. Chuck had quickly become a favorite with ranchers and horse enthusiasts. Whenever he came to tend to Lancelot—which was only a couple of times a year—she got to spend a few minutes chatting with him and then spent weeks going over the conversation in her mind.

He set Lancelot's hoof down gently and patted his shoulder. "I really don't see anything wrong. Why don't we wrap this overnight? You can call me if he's limping tomorrow."

"Okay." She held the halter firmly while Chuck got out a bandage and wound it around the horse's pastern and cannon. Lancelot nickered, and Ruby stroked his long, smooth cheek.

"All set." Chuck stood and smiled at her over Lancelot's withers.

Right there. That smile. That was what put her in a dither. Last year they'd both attended a picnic for the volunteers working at the Wyoming 100. That was when she'd first begun to imagine Chuck liked her, too. But she'd been so busy all winter, and her horse was so annoyingly healthy, that their paths had only crossed a few times since. He'd given Lancelot a complete checkup in the spring before she began intense training for the hundred-mile ride, and she'd seen him twice over the summer—once at a horse show and again in the foreign foods section of the grocery store, of all places, where they'd discovered they both loved Chinese food. She'd wondered at the time if he thought he was too old for her—there must be six or seven years' difference in their ages. But neither of them was a kid anymore, and the older they got, the less that would matter.

"I guess we're done." Chuck was still smiling at her, as though he almost wished he had more to do at the Dales' house today.

"Great. That's a gorgeous Appaloosa you've got, Chuck. I hope you have a good time at the ride."

"I expect I'll see you there."

"Yeah, I guess you will." Brainless comment. Why couldn't she come up with something better? She unsnapped the cross ties and led Lancelot out to the paddock. When she had let him go and closed the gate, she turned and saw Chuck standing by his pickup. She walked over, her pulse fluttering at the thought that he was waiting to speak to her again.

"Hey, I was thinking." He looked off toward the hills and laughed. "Something I do now and then."

"Really?" She couldn't help laughing, too.

"Yeah. And I was wondering why we couldn't do a training ride together sometime. Assuming Lancelot's none the worse for his little incident today, I mean. I want to take Rascal for a nice long ramble in the hills—say thirty or forty miles."

"That would be a great warm-up for the 100." She bit her bottom lip. He'd just asked her to spend a day with him. She felt the heat climbing her cheekbones. "It would be fun."

"That's what I thought. We did twenty this morning, but Rascal needs a few lengthier practice rides." He eyed her for a long moment, and she waited. "Could you do it next weekend if your horse is all right?"

"Yeah, I think so."

"Great." There was the dazzling smile again. Ruby had to look away. "I could come by with the double trailer, and we could drive up toward Powder River and start our ride there. What do you think?"

"Fantastic. It would give Lancelot and me some new scenery to look at. How about if I pack a lunch?"

"Sounds good. But be sure to tell me if there's any problem with Lancelot. We don't want to take any chances with him."

"I will." She hoped desperately Lancelot wouldn't show any signs of pain tomorrow.

Chuck nodded and opened his truck door, smiling.

Ruby watched him drive out and waved as he pulled onto the road. Chuck waved back. She exhaled and looked over toward the paddock. Lancelot was rolling, all four feet thrashing, as he flopped back and forth on the turf. Ruby went over and leaned on the fence. "Did you hear that? We've got a date next weekend."

Lancelot rolled to his stomach and pushed himself up, front end first, then his hindquarters. He shook his head and shuddered all over, sending dust and bits of grass flying from his coat then pranced over to the fence and whinnied.

"You big baby." Ruby scratched his forehead, beneath his white forelock, and looked down the road in the direction Chuck had driven. She turned back to the horse. "I can't believe he finally asked me out. And for a trail ride. Does it get any better than this?"

❧

Chuck pulled into the yard at the Dale home early the next Saturday, anticipating an enjoyable outing but at the same time a little nervous. He hadn't dated anyone seriously since moving to the area, although several women had tried to snare his attention.

Seeing Martin Dale sitting in a rocker on the front porch didn't help. It struck Chuck that Ruby's father was watchdogging his daughter's social life—and Chuck was cast as the suspicious intruder.

"Good morning, Mr. Dale," he called as he exited the truck.

Ruby's father stood and came to the top of the porch steps, holding a white china mug. "Morning, Dr. Sullivan."

Chuck smiled as he walked toward him. "Please, call me Chuck."

"All right then. Ruby says you're going riding up in the hills today."

"Yes, sir. We're both training for the Wyoming 100, so I thought we could give the horses a workout together."

Mr. Dale nodded, his eyes slightly narrowed. "I suppose you know the trails up there."

"Not very well, but they're clearly marked."

"Well, Ruby's a good rider."

"I'm sure she is, sir."

Mr. Dale grunted and sipped his coffee.

"I assume Lancelot is all right," Chuck said. "Ruby said on Monday he seemed fine."

"Yes, she babied him for a couple of days, but she was saying last night he seemed right as rain."

"Great. Uh. . .is Ruby ready to go?"

"She's in the barn. You had breakfast?"

"Yes, I have. Thank you."

Her father nodded again and jerked his head toward the barn. "She's been out there for an hour. That palomino must be shiny enough so's you can see your face in his hide."

Chuck laughed. "She takes good care of him. Every time I see Lancelot, he looks like a pampered and contented horse."

"You'll watch out for her?"

"Of course."

"I suppose I sound like a meddling old nanny, but we don't know you very well, Doc."

Chuck gulped and tried not to let his smile slip as he took a step closer to him. "Sir, you don't have to worry about Ruby with me."

Their gazes locked for a moment, and her father pursed his lips. "All right then. Call me Martin." He shifted his coffee mug and extended his right hand. Chuck shook it solemnly, determined to live up to the implied promise.

Measured hoofbeats behind him told him Ruby and Lancelot had emerged from the barn. He turned just as Rascal let out a piercing whinny from inside the trailer.

"Hi," Ruby called, holding the lead rope firmly as Lancelot tossed his head and nickered, his ears pricked toward Chuck's rig. The palomino's rounded flanks really did gleam in the sunlight. Ruby looked ready to hit the trail in faded jeans and a blue-and-white striped T-shirt, topped by a denim jacket. Her glossy hair was caught back in a braid.

"Good morning. How's he doing?"

"He's fine," Ruby said. "Eager to go."

As Chuck walked around to lower the ramp on the trailer, Ruby's mother pushed open the screen door and came out of the house to stand beside Martin.

"Hello, Dr. Sullivan. I thought I heard you drive in. You two are getting an early start. Or should I say, 'you four'?"

Chuck laughed. "You're up early yourself, Mrs. Dale." It wasn't quite seven, the time he and Ruby had agreed on.

"It's hard to sleep in on Saturday when you're up early all week." She smiled at her daughter. "Want me to bring out your lunch cooler, honey?"

"That would be great, Mom."

Chuck reached for the lead rope. "I'll load him, unless you want to."

Ruby surrendered the lead, and Lancelot whickered, spewing a few drops of saliva on Chuck's shirt. Chuck spoke to him and patted his neck, and the horse went calmly up the ramp with him. A moment later Lancelot was secure beside Rascal, who pulled his head around as far as his tie-up would allow to inspect the newcomer.

Chuck left the trailer and found Martin ready to help him swing up the ramp. Ruby and her mother were settling a soft pack in the back of his pickup.

"I'll get your tack," Martin said and hurried to the barn. He returned with Ruby's saddle, blanket, and bridle, which Chuck stowed next to his own gear in the truck bed. They all said good-bye, and Chuck rounded the front of the truck with Ruby to open the passenger door for her. He realized how short she was—not quite to his shoulder. He offered his hand for a boost. She glanced at him with a quick smile, took his hand, and pushed against it for leverage as she swung up into the cab.

On the way to their destination Ruby was very quiet at first. As soon as he'd checked in his mirrors to be sure the trailer was rolling smoothly, Chuck looked over at her. "Thanks for coming. Sometimes I get kind of lonesome on the trail with nobody but Rascal to talk to."

A dainty dimple appeared at the corner of her smile. "Thanks for asking me. I usually ride alone now, and my folks worry about me."

"No kidding."

She laughed at his "could have fooled me" tone. "Yeah, they're afraid Lancelot will dump me somewhere and come back with an empty saddle."

"Well, some parents are a little overprotective." He glanced at her again. Her expression had gone sober.

"I guess they're allowed," she said. "I keep telling myself I need to move away from home and get a life, but I love Mom and Dad. And I know they'd miss me."

"Are you an only child?"

She hesitated. "I am now."

So. That explained a lot of things. The Dales kept their surviving child close. "I'm sorry," he said softly. They rode along in silence for a few minutes, and he was sure he'd put his foot in it.

As they passed a horse ranch, Ruby caught her breath. "Oh, look!" Several yearling colts raced each other across the broad pasture, heads held high and tails flying.

"I was out there a couple of weeks ago," Chuck said. "One of the mares was lame."

"I envy you." Her eyes were gentle brown, almost golden.

He looked away, straight ahead, but he could still picture them. "Why is that?"

"You get to work with animals, and you must be outside a lot on the job."

"Yeah, sometimes when I wish I could stay home. Rain, sleet, or snow I'm out there."

She chuckled, and his heart lurched. Her momentary sadness had passed, and she was ready to embark on a lighter thread of conversation.

"At least you have an interesting job." He hoped she would continue to talk. He liked the quiet flow of her voice.

"Yes, I admit it's not dull. But I sit there for hours with headphones on, taking calls. Fender benders, domestic disputes, prowlers, shoplifters. We get to take breaks, but sometimes it's so busy I forget. I usually go out of the police station on my supper break, though, just for a change of scenery and to stretch my legs."

"That's a good idea for people with sedentary jobs."

She nodded. "Yeah. But since I work from four in the afternoon until 2:00 a.m., it's dark out at suppertime after we turn the clocks back."

"You get off at two o'clock in the morning? That's a long shift."

"Yeah. I do four 'tens' a week. The officers are good about escorting us to our cars when we change shifts, so the security part of it doesn't bother me. Sometimes I get sleepy toward the end, though, and then I have to drive home late. But I do like having most of my days free. I can ride for an hour or two just about every day and more on my off days."

"I hear you. It's been hard for me to carve out the time, but I love riding."

They'd reached the foothills. He pulled in to a grassy place off the road. Two other vehicles were parked there, one with an empty ATV trailer behind it.

"I'll bet the horses will be glad to get out and have a look at each other," Ruby said.

Chuck smiled at that and tried to imagine being tied up

in a trailer beside a stranger and having to ride next to him. He got out of the pickup. Ruby met him at the back of the rig, and he lowered the ramp. When their owners unhitched them, both horses backed down to solid ground, whinnying to each other. Chuck showed Ruby where to tie Lancelot securely. He hooked Rascal to a rope on the other side of the trailer, and they both saddled up.

"Did you want to take the lunch along or come back here for it?" Ruby asked when the horses were ready. "I put everything in a small insulated pack to keep the drinks and things cold, but Lancelot can carry it behind his saddle if you want."

"Okay, let's do that." Chuck brought it from the truck. It was fairly heavy, but the horse didn't flinch when he set it gently behind the cantle of the saddle.

"You use a English saddle," he said in surprise. "I'm sure I saw a Western saddle in your barn last week."

Ruby shrugged. "This is lighter. When we're going on a long ride, I like to keep the weight down, for Lancelot's sake." She strapped on the pack. "I take my lunch with me in this cooler sometimes. It's great not to have to hurry back and to have a cold drink and something to eat when you get ten miles from home and realize you're starving." She walked forward to unhitch Lancelot and reached down to grab her baseball cap from the trailer's fender. After settling it over her rich brown hair, she gathered the reins and lifted her left foot to the stirrup. In an instant she was sitting astride, smiling down at him. "All set?"

Chuck was still looking at her scuffed white running shoes and calculating how much lighter his gear would be if he switched to an English saddle and left his boots home. But the week before his first hundred-miler wasn't the time to change equipment.

"Yeah, sure." He unclipped Rascal from the trailer and mounted. The trail they chose rose gradually at first, and they trotted along together then slowed as the incline increased. The sprinkling of trees on the rolling hills became denser as they progressed along the trail. The foliage was turning color on the hardwoods. Chuck inhaled deeply. He loved this time of year.

Ruby reached out and plucked a golden leaf from an aspen as she passed, rolled the stem back and forth between her fingers a few times then let the leaf flutter to the earth. When the track narrowed, Chuck let her lead the way. Her palomino had a nice rhythm, and Ruby sat easily in the saddle, obviously comfortable.

A steep grade slowed their pace, and after a while Ruby hopped down.

She turned and walked backward beside her horse for a moment, holding his reins. "I'm going to walk up this one."

Chuck climbed down, too, and Rascal lowered his head with a snuffle, plodding up the slope behind Lancelot.

They came out on a rounded knob above the tree line. Ruby led Lancelot to a fairly flat spot and stood looking out over the plain below. Chuck eased Rascal over beside them.

"Terrific view."

She turned toward him. "Isn't it great? I've never been up here before. You can see clear out across the plains."

"You ride very well."

"Thanks." She looked down and fiddled with the reins she held.

"How long have you had Lancelot?"

"About five years. I bought him while I was still in college. I stayed home and commuted."

He nodded, thinking it must have been nice to be able to afford college *and* a good horse.

Her rueful chuckle squelched the thought. "It's probably why I can't afford my own apartment."

"Horsemanship is an expensive sport." He let Rascal put his head down and crop the drying grass.

"Well, it's been a sort of compensation for me."

"Oh?"

She looked up at him, and that sober, faraway look returned to her eyes. "My twin sister and I went to Cornell University together our first year. Pre-med. But. . .there was an accident. A car crash. It wasn't her fault, but. . .after Julie died, my parents wanted me to stay close."

He nodded, trying to put the pieces together.

"Anyway, Dad said it would mean a lot to them, especially to Mom, to have me nearby. But they figured I'd be giving up a lot. They offered to help me buy a good horse." She sucked her upper lip into her mouth for a moment. "But living here and going to the community college was a lot cheaper than the university, so I guess we've all saved money in the long run. Probably for the best." Her frown belied her words.

"It's been rough for your family."

"Yeah." She puffed out a breath and smiled. "But God knows what He's doing. I believe that."

Her gaze met his, and Chuck nodded. "I do, too. Are things getting better now?"

"Some. The pain never goes away, you know?"

"Yeah, I do." A memory of his father's gentle face flitted across his mind.

After a moment she looked over the knoll. "Do you want to keep going? This trail seems to go down a ways, but I think it goes up that ridge over there." She pointed to the next hill.

"Sure, if you're game."

"Let's go." She positioned her reins and put her foot in the stirrup to mount.

Chuck pulled Rascal's head up and swung into the saddle. He liked Ruby. So far she'd lived up to his expectations. Frank, no-nonsense, direct. Cute. Great horsewoman. Very cute. Her golden brown braid bounced against the back of her denim jacket. In spite of her delicate frame she had a toughness. She would fall into the featherweight class for certain at the ride while Chuck figured he'd hit middleweight with all his gear at the weigh-in. But despite her small stature Ruby would never be one to shirk her own stable chores. Chuck liked that. He liked the fact that she trusted God with her future, too, no matter how bleak things must have seemed for a while.

The horses wended downward then entered a cool stretch of conifer forest. A magpie flew across the trail from a low-hanging spruce branch, and Lancelot shied but settled down under Ruby's firm hand. When they emerged from the woods fifteen minutes later, the path widened. Chuck trotted his Appaloosa up beside Ruby and Lancelot. She looked over at him.

Without giving much thought to his words, Chuck said, "Yeah, this is a lot better than riding alone."

His momentary fear that he'd been too forward was erased in the glow of Ruby's smile.

two

The day with Chuck was as close to a perfect day as Ruby could remember. They ate their sandwiches, vegetable sticks, and cookies at a camp spot near the trail and let the horses graze while they talked. By the end of that half hour she'd lost a little of her shyness with him, though she still felt under-qualified in his presence.

She'd aspired to medical school once—for people, not animals, but she knew vet school was as difficult and perhaps more competitive. Chuck had made it through. She hadn't. She'd had to switch majors when she left the university. Instead of pre-med she took a bachelor's degree in humanities. She wished now she'd taken a vocational course, but at the time she'd been too numb to concentrate on the future.

Not that she minded her job at the police station. She helped stop crime indirectly and had even received credit for helping save the life of a young woman who called in a medical emergency. But it was a job, not a career. Ruby couldn't see herself sitting before the communications console at the station for another forty years. Sometimes she wished she'd taken criminal justice and become a police officer. In the five years since Julie's death she'd avoided making long-term decisions. But maybe it was time.

"I'm not too old to go back to school," she told Chuck as they rode slowly back down the trail toward the truck.

His eyebrows shot up as he looked over at her. "Well, sure. Even medical school, if you still want to."

His quick affirmation brought a smidgen of comfort. Spending an entire day with Chuck Sullivan had given her much to mull over. She'd learned more about him, and all of it was good—his family in Laramie, his struggle to put himself through college and graduate school, his great relationship with his mom and siblings. The only bad part was his father's death from a heart attack fifteen years ago.

He was a good enough rider to compete in the Wyoming 100, and he took excellent care of his mount. No need to worry about his pushing Rascal too hard. Some riders new to the sport asked more than their horses could give, but Chuck wouldn't.

As he turned his pickup in at her family's driveway, she watched his sturdy hands on the wheel and the way he automatically checked the trailer in the side view mirror. Detail oriented. . .steady. . .diligent. . .handsome. He pulled up in front of the barn.

"Thanks, Chuck. I had a really good time today."

"Me, too. I think getting a horse has been good for me. And riding with you was good for me, too."

She ducked her head, feeling a blush warm her cheeks.

"Are you planning to help set up for the 100 next Friday?" he asked. "I think you said you don't work Friday."

"Right. I'm planning to be there."

"I'm going to try to go, too. If I'm not swamped with patients, I'll see you there. But I'll be there for sure at the riders' meeting and campfire that night."

She couldn't hold in her smile, but she didn't want to try. "That's great." He opened his truck door, and she pulled the latch on hers and hopped down. Too late, she realized he was going around the front of the truck to help her down, not heading directly to the trailer.

"Uh, thanks." She glanced up at him then away.

He laughed. "I guess that's a good sign."

"What?"

"You're not used to having a gentleman do things for you."

"Not very often."

He nodded. "Like I said, that's good. . .for me."

She wondered suddenly how many women he'd squired around. Not many since he came to live here, she was sure. In a small town like this she'd have heard rumors.

They walked to the trailer, and he lowered the ramp.

"I can get Lancelot," she said.

"Okay, I'll get your tack."

When she'd backed her horse down the ramp, Chuck was waiting near the barn door, carrying her saddle. Rascal pawed inside the trailer and whinnied. Lancelot answered him and pulled at the lead line.

"Settle down." Ruby walked him to the barn door and into the dim interior. The familiar smells of hay, sweet feed, leather, and manure greeted her. She walked him into his box stall and released him. Lancelot whinnied again and shook his white mane.

"Relax, would ya? I'll get your supper in a minute." She put her hand to his throat to get a quick count of his pulse. Slow and steady.

Chuck was waiting for her just outside the stall, grinning. "I think he and Rascal bonded."

"For sure."

"I put your tack away."

"Thanks."

They walked to the truck, and he hefted the lunch pack out.

"Are you camping at the ride site next Friday?"

"I don't think so. I know most of the riders do, but I live so close I figured I'd go over early Saturday morning. Lancelot will sleep better in his own stall that night."

Chuck nodded. "That's what I decided to do. They said we could do the preliminary vet check-in Saturday morning if we got there early."

The house door opened, and her mother came onto the porch.

"Hi. Did you have a good time?"

"Yeah, it was great," Ruby called. She glanced at Chuck in apology, but it didn't seem to bother him that her folks hovered. They walked over to the steps.

"Did you have a good day, Mrs. Dale?" Chuck asked.

"Yes, I made applesauce and cleaned the hall closet."

Ruby smiled at her mother's idea of fun. "We had a good workout."

"The horses did, too," Chuck added with a grin.

Her mother laughed. "Would you like to stay for supper?"

Chuck glanced at Ruby. "Well, I ought to get over to the office for a while and see if Dr. Hogan had any emergencies. He told me he wouldn't call me today, but I should check in with him."

"Another time," Ruby's mother said.

Ruby didn't look at him, so Chuck nodded and murmured, "Thank you. Ruby, if all goes well I'll see you next week at the setup."

"Right. Thanks again for today."

Chuck smiled at them both and turned toward his truck. Ruby could feel a barrage of questions coming on from her mother.

"I need to feed and water Lancelot." She hurried toward the barn.

On Wednesday afternoon Ruby took her place in the police station's communications center, a few feet away from the other evening dispatcher, Nadine Carter. They shared most of their overlapping shifts, but Nadine had been on duty an hour when Ruby checked in. This system prevented them from losing track of situations in progress when the dispatchers changed.

Nadine finished a call and turned to face Ruby. "Pretty quiet today. I'm monitoring a traffic stop on Antelope Street and a domestic call in town."

Ruby nodded and reached for her headphones. "Thanks." She settled into her padded chair. The next few hours were moderately busy, with routine calls. She answered questions and directed officers to respond to requests. In the slower moments she let her thoughts stray to Chuck. He'd called her last night, "just because," and she was still smiling over that. He'd confessed he'd rescheduled a few routine procedures for bovine patients in order to increase his chances of seeing her on Friday. Not "helping set up for the ride," she'd noted. "Seeing you." That was enough to keep her head in the clouds.

The patrol sergeant's sudden intrusion brought her swiftly to earth.

"Dispatch, we have a high-risk situation," called Sergeant Harrison's voice in her headphones. "I need you to track detectives Austin and Wheeler." He gave the numerical code for a drug-related incident. Ruby's mind clicked into focus, and all thoughts of Chuck and the ride fled.

"Got it." Ruby tapped the officers' badge numbers into her computer. The system would give her an electronic tone every five minutes to remind her to check on them.

Over the next hour the incident evolved into a major surveillance operation. The two detectives and three uniformed officers took up positions where they could observe an isolated private airstrip, hoping to catch drug runners when they landed their plane.

The officers performed their status checks on schedule, giving her a "status quo" report each time. Austin's voice sounded more and more sleepy as time passed. It was a fairly boring exercise for Ruby as well, but she knew if the plane landed things would get busy in a hurry.

As the hour grew later she felt her energy droop and went for a cup of coffee. At one o'clock Nadine's relief came in. Ruby told the graveyard shift dispatcher, Larry Tivoli, about the case she was tracking, and he took over Nadine's console and her ongoing incidents.

Just before 2:00 a.m. Ruby's relief dispatcher arrived. The detectives were still checking in faithfully, but the plane they were waiting for hadn't arrived. Ruby turned her headphones over and headed home, eager for some sleep. She considered grabbing another cup of coffee, but if she did that she'd be wired and unable to sleep for hours. She was glad the drive home was only four miles.

*

"I think I can give you Friday off again," Dr. Hogan said genially as he lifted a Scottish terrier out of his kennel in the veterinary office. "You covered for me all day yesterday. And the whole town knows the office will be closed Saturday because we'll both be at the ride. Everyone needs a day off sometime to have fun, right?"

Chuck grinned. "Right. Everybody will know where to find us the day of the 100. Thanks, John."

The older man smiled and set the small dog carefully on

the examining table. "There, Hamish, are you feeling better this morning?" He put his stethoscope to the dog's rib cage.

Chuck glanced over his schedule for the day. Two house calls at ranches this morning and office hours after lunch. Not bad.

He drove to the first appointment, a ranch where he was scheduled to vaccinate a small herd of Angus cattle. After an hour with the rancher he headed to the Riley home. Fifteen-year-old Rebecca Riley's barrel-racing horse had pulled up lame during practice two days earlier. Chuck had treated the mare, Shasta, and advised Rebecca to keep the horse in a box stall so she would rest, dose the leg with liniment, and rewrap it daily.

A young blond woman he recognized as Rebecca's older sister, Claire, met him in the yard as soon as he pulled in. Chuck grabbed his veterinary bag and climbed out of the truck. "Good morning, Claire. How's Shasta doing?"

"Becky says she's better. She wanted to stay home from school so she'd be here when you came, but our mom made her go. I told Becky I'd make sure Shasta got the best treatment."

Chuck smiled, but he wished Becky, or even her mother, were present. Claire made him nervous. She'd deluged him with cookies and invitations to community events when he'd first arrived in town. She was pretty, but her aggressive manner put him off.

Claire led him into the barn and leaned on the bottom half of the stall's Dutch door while he examined Shasta's leg.

"Oh, that feels much better," he said. "No heat in it today. Would you mind walking her out for me so I can watch her stride?"

"Sure." Claire clipped a lead rope to Shasta's halter and led her into the alleyway and out toward the driveway. Chuck tried not to notice how tight Claire's leggings were. He concentrated on the horse's steps and the way Shasta placed her weight evenly on each foot as she walked.

"Great," he called. "She's bearing weight on it. Turn her around."

Claire walked the horse back toward him. "Tell Becky I said to give her another day of rest before she rides her, okay? And no barrel racing for another week. That's too stressful. I'll come back next week to check Shasta over, and if she's okay then, I'll give Becky the green light for practice again."

"She'll miss the competition in Casper next weekend." Claire led Shasta back into the box stall and removed the lead rope.

"I'm sorry about that, but it's better than doing permanent damage to her horse's leg."

"Right. I'll remind her of that." Claire smiled at him as she emerged from the stall. "How about a cup of coffee, Chuck? I've got a fresh pot in the kitchen, and I made some brownies."

Uneasy prickles skittered over Chuck's arms. Why did Claire make him feel so. . .stalked? Ruby never gave him that sensation.

"Thanks, but I have office hours coming up. I need to get back to town."

She raised her chin. "Maybe another time."

He almost said, "Sure," but caught himself. Even that generic response might cause her to claim later he'd made a promise. "Uh. . .maybe. Thanks for the offer." He climbed in his truck and drove away feeling as though he'd escaped an unpleasant experience. He supposed Claire wasn't so bad, but she'd come on so strong ever since he'd met her that she'd killed any natural inclination on his part to get to know her better.

Now Ruby was another story. She was quiet, perhaps even a bit reserved, but she had substance. Yes, she cared about animals, but she cared about people, too. The ease he felt in her presence was worlds away from the fidgets Claire gave him. He flipped the radio on and hummed as he drove, thinking of Ruby in her sneakers and baseball cap. Not a glamour girl, but perhaps something better. He wanted to find out.

❧

When she arrived at work Thursday afternoon Ruby felt better. She'd slept until noon, and then she'd taken Lancelot out for an hour-long workout, riding around a large ranch that belonged to the Dales' easterly neighbors. The ride energized her and increased her anticipation for the upcoming hundred-mile contest. Lancelot was at his peak, and the ride was only two days away.

She sank into her padded swivel chair behind the console unable to stop envisioning what tomorrow would bring. She planned to arrive early at the ride start, ready to post markers, set up checkpoints, or anything else the committee needed. And Chuck would be there. Well, probably. She sent up a quick prayer that he would have no emergencies and be able to take part in the setup fun. She refused to consider the letdown that awaited her if he couldn't make it.

Nadine signed off on a call and turned her chair. "Hi."

"How's it going?" Ruby asked.

"A little busy."

"Did that plane ever come in last night?"

"No, the detectives stayed out until 5:00 a.m., and it never showed. Oops." She swiveled quickly back to the console and answered another call.

Ruby went to the duty room to stow her purse in the locker

she'd been assigned. Officer Nelson Flagg was working at one of the computer stations but glanced up at her.

"Howdy, Ruby."

"Hello, Nels. How's the baby?"

"Good."

She closed her locker door and pushed her hair back. "Everything going okay today?"

"Yeah, except the detectives are moaning about those cocaine runners they thought they were going to nab last night. Seems their reliable tipster isn't so reliable after all."

Ruby grimaced at him. "That's too bad. I know Detective Austin was counting on making some arrests."

Flagg nodded. "We all want to stop the drugs from coming into the county. But they've been trying for months and haven't succeeded in catching the dealers."

"I know. Maybe they'll find out what went wrong and get another chance."

"Let's hope so."

three

Ruby's Jeep spun dust clouds behind her as she drove the dirt road to the ranch where the ride would begin. The owner allowed the sponsoring horsemen's club to use one of his back fields as the start area every year. It was only a mile from a campground many of the contestants used. The club had built a wood-framed booth for the ride officials and a small storage shed on the edge of the field. Riders, their vehicles, the veterinary check-in post and spectators would fill the area tomorrow, but now there were only a few SUVs and pickups. She parked and climbed out, pulling on her baseball cap.

"Good morning, Ruby!"

She smiled and joined Hester Marden, an energetic woman who was a mainstay of the club. Hester and her husband, Tom, both in their fifties, raised Paso Finos.

"Looks like we're early birds," Ruby said.

"Yes, but they're trickling in. I think we'll have a good group to put up the markers today." Hester nodded toward the gray pickup entering the field. "There's Jeffrey Tavish."

"Last year's winner," Ruby noted. She'd never actually met him but had watched him win the trophy.

"Mm. Second time in a row," Hester said.

"He's a good rider."

"Oh, yes, and a good trainer. He deserves all the ribbons he wins. And he rode in the 100 for five years before he worked his way up to first place. I'd say he's earned his laurels." Hester nudged her as Jeff got out of his truck. "Not bad looking either."

Ruby smiled. "Come on, Hester. What if Tom hears you talking like that?"

Hester laughed. "Oh, he can take it. Say, there's Sandy Larkin. I need to see her. The check for my club dues hasn't cleared the bank yet." Hester strode off to buttonhole the club treasurer.

Ruby looked around and spotted a few more people she knew from the club and from helping with the ride in previous years. As she chatted with the ride secretary, Jeff Tavish joined them.

"Looks like we've got a good crew today," Jeff said.

"Yes." The secretary, Allison Bowie, surveyed the gathering. "I expect we'll get everything done before suppertime."

Jeff gazed at Ruby with twinkling gray eyes. "You look familiar. Have we met?"

"I've helped out the last few years," Ruby said.

"She's one of our best workers," Allison told him. "You must have met Ruby."

"No, I think I'd remember. Suppose you introduce us."

Ruby felt her color rise as Jeff continued to watch her. She didn't know much about him, except that he'd mastered the art of endurance riding and took excellent care of his horses.

"Ruby Dale, meet Jeff Tavish," Allison said with a bit of a drawl.

Jeff lifted his Stetson and extended his other hand. "Very pleased to meet you, Ruby."

She shook his hand briefly. "Thanks. Are you going to defend your title?"

"I'm surely going to try." He definitely wasn't bad looking— dark blond hair that fluttered in the breeze, a long face set in a solemn expression belied by his laughing eyes. "Will you be helping at one of the checkpoints tomorrow?"

Allison laughed and swatted at his arm. "No, she won't. She's competing this year, and I've seen her horse. She'll give you a run for your money, Jeff."

He nodded, surveying Ruby with new respect. "I look forward to it."

From the corner of her eye Ruby saw a black pickup pulling into the field. She didn't want Chuck's first glimpse of her to also be one of Jeff Tavish.

"Have you made up the assignments for today, Allison?" she asked.

"Tom Marden's taking care of that."

"Well then, if you'll excuse me, I think I'll go see where I'm needed." She nodded at Jeff and Allison and walked quickly to the knot of people near the officials' booth. As she had hoped, Chuck was also approaching the group.

He smiled when he spotted her and diverted his steps in her direction.

"You made it!" She couldn't help the cheerleader smile that sprang to her lips. The answering glint in his eyes set her pulse thudding.

"Yes, I'm free for the day. Do we know what we're doing yet?"

"Tom Marden is starting to give assignments, but I think a lot of people went to the campground first to leave their gear." She and Chuck edged up to the back of the small crowd and listened as Tom described each chore and wrote down the names of those who volunteered to see the job done.

"For those of you who want to stay close to base camp today, we need volunteers to set up for the barbecue," Tom called. "Dick and Loreta Halstead will be in charge of the food, but I'm sure they could use an assistant or two, and we need to set up tables and so on. The riders' meeting and campfire will be held over at the campground, immediately after the barbecue."

Several people stepped forward to volunteer.

"Now, folks," Tom said after a few minutes, "this year we're changing the route a little bit. We got permission to follow the old stagecoach road in the hills for a few miles."

"Yes, and it's a beautiful section of trail," Allison said, and Ruby realized the secretary and Jeff were standing near her and Chuck.

Tom nodded. "We'll pick it up at Mile 56, after the second bridge. It's pretty good footing."

"Wasn't that road abandoned back when they built the new highway?" one of the men asked.

"That's right," Tom said. "It's as crooked as a snake, but it should be safe enough for horses. Since we haven't used that stretch before we need all new markings for several miles, but it's not a terribly difficult section. It will loop around and hit our regular route at the old Mile 59, which will now be Mile 63. We're moving the sixty-mile checkpoint down there to even things out a little, but that stretch between checks will still be a long one. And after that, of course, all the mile markers need to be adjusted. We're taking out the loop around Pikes' ranch, and the finish line will be about a mile east of where it was last year."

Chuck looked down at Ruby. "Want to do the new part?"

"Sure."

Chuck raised his hand. "Tom, we'll take the new section. Me and Ruby."

Ruby could feel Jeff's intent gaze on her. She glanced over, and sure enough he was watching her. It was flattering to think he was interested in her, but her heart had room only for Chuck these days. She flashed Jeff a quick smile and turned her attention back to what Tom was saying.

"Right, Chuck. You can drive up to the bridge and start there. It's only about twenty-five miles from here by the road, even though it's at Mile 56 on the trail. Our route for the 100 loops around and switches back through the hills."

Chuck accepted a sheet of paper and a roll of orange surveyors' tape from Hester, who was assisting her husband at assigning the jobs. Hester handed Ruby a sheaf of laminated arrow signs and showed them on the printed map where to post the arrows and ribbon markers.

"Want to take my Jeep?" Ruby asked, looking up into Chuck's blue eyes.

"Sure, if you want."

As they walked toward the parked vehicle, Ruby spotted Jeff in the center of a group of laughing people. She was glad he'd found some congenial companions.

With Chuck sitting beside her in the Jeep she found it difficult to concentrate on the winding trail. He held their supplies on his lap and watched eagerly out the window as she drove.

"I love riding in this area," he said, "but it's a little far from home. I've only managed to bring Rascal up here once, and we did the first six miles of the ride route, up and back."

"That's a start," Ruby said. "At least he'll recognize the beginning. That will probably help him feel at ease."

"I hope so. He loved being out on the trail with you and Lancelot last week, but he'll have more than fifty other horses around him when we come here tomorrow."

"True. Amazing how this ride has grown over the last few years." Ruby slowed the Jeep as she maneuvered a sharp turn. "I'm glad we can drive some parts of the trail. It makes the setup easier. But I know I'll love the remote parts best. It's great getting out away from civilization on a horse, where you know you won't meet any cars."

"I agree. But I hope we don't have to walk the whole seven miles of our section and back."

Ruby grinned and jerked her head toward the backseat. "I did pack a few sandwiches. I figured we'd need something between now and supper."

Chuck's jaw dropped. "You mean we *are* going to walk fourteen miles today?"

"No, but probably five or six."

He bobbed his head back and forth as though weighing that. "I guess I can handle it. I got a little smarter and wore my running shoes today."

After a half-hour drive she parked the Jeep at the side of the trail before the log bridge at Mile 56. When the competitors reached this point they would have to cross the narrow span to continue the ride.

"We'll have to walk in from here and flag the next mile or so," she told him, "but then we can come back and take the Jeep around the mountain. There's an access road off the highway. I volunteered at the checkpoint up there last year."

Chuck studied the crude map Tom had given him. "I think I see it. This dotted line?"

"Yeah. It's not a great road, but we can get the job done. This loop here, though—from about Mile 61 to the end of our section. . ." She pointed on the map. "We'll have to walk that part, too. But the scenery should be spectacular."

"Right." He smiled at her. "I guess we can drive around to the other end of the stagecoach road and walk in for that part."

"That's what I figure. We'll do that section last."

Chuck picked up his pile of signs, tape, and a hammer. "Ready anytime you are, Dr. Livingstone."

Her stomach fluttered as she folded the map and tucked it in her pocket. She had definitely drawn the best chore today.

The task took longer than Ruby had anticipated, and she realized they would be riding over some very rugged terrain during the race.

"What's the record time for this ride?" Chuck asked as he cut several strips of orange tape with his pocketknife.

"Fifteen hours and twenty-nine minutes, held by Jeff Tavish. Do you know him?"

"He's not one of Doc Hogan's and my clients, but I met him last year at the ride. He had a fantastic Arabian–quarter horse cross. He didn't get the best conditioned award, but he came close, if I remember correctly."

"You probably do. Jeff lives in Casper. He's the defending champion, and he's here today." She hesitated. "Well, not right here now. I mean he came for the setup. I saw him for a minute this morning."

They finished the first part of their assignment and drove by little-used trails up to the spot where the Mile 63 checkpoint would be. From there they drove as far as they could, posting arrows and hanging ribbons on branches.

"Getting hungry?" she asked.

Chuck looked at his watch. "Yeah. It's after one. Why don't we eat before we do the last part where we have to walk in?"

They found a spot on a ridge where they could sit to eat their sandwiches looking out over the valley. "That's the Medicine Bow River." Ruby pointed to the stream far in the distance. Between them and the river the land sloped down, with abrupt falls from cliffs and rock outcroppings. Deep ravines cut between the summits, and spruce trees stood stiff and spiky, with little underbrush beneath them.

"I hope I get through this part before dark tomorrow,"

Chuck said. "They really should have railings on some of the curves up here."

Movement between the trees beneath their high perch caught Ruby's eye. "Look. Someone's riding down there."

"Where?" Chuck leaned over behind her and sighted along her arm as she pointed.

Ruby felt his breath move her hair, and a prickle slid down her spine. "Down there, to the left of that boulder."

"I see them." He straightened and squinted down at the figures. "Looks like two horses."

"I thought at first they were elk," Ruby said, "but the riders are leading them."

"It's great weather for it. Cool, but not too chilly."

"Don't remind me about what's coming in a couple of months." Ruby ate the last of her sandwich. "Want a brownie?"

"Sure. I didn't know I was getting a two-course meal."

She laughed and reached into her day pack. "Just light refreshments. The real feed is later." She glanced up at him. "You're staying for the barbecue, right?"

"Wouldn't miss it." He accepted one of the fudge brownies and looked down into the ravine again. "Hey, look. They've tied up their horses."

Ruby frowned and focused on the tiny figures below them again. "There's a rockslide or something over there."

"Probably too rough for the horses," Chuck agreed. "I wonder if they're just out hiking, or if they have something to do with the ride."

"That area looks too rugged for the ride. Even though they make it tough, riding in terrain like that would be dangerous." Ruby looked at her watch. "Guess we'd better get moving."

Chuck stood and offered her a hand up. "Okay, we can't drive any farther."

"Right," Ruby said. "We'll have to do this last part of the stagecoach road on foot. At the rate we're going, it will probably take us at least a couple of hours to finish." She stooped to brush off her jeans.

"We've got plenty of time."

Two hours later Ruby scrambled down a sharp incline clutching the few remaining arrow signs.

"This is really steep, Chuck. Are you sure we took the right fork back there?"

"Well. . .I was thinking we should have hit the main trail again by now. This looks dangerous, doesn't it?" He eyed the drop-off at the edge of the narrow path. "Let's make sure." He fished the map out of his shirt pocket and smoothed it out.

Ruby climbed back up to stand beside him. They both bent over the map, and she was aware once again of his nearness as his masculine scent tickled her nose. She made herself think about the trail, not her charming companion.

"See? Right here." She pointed on the map to the last place where they'd posted an arrow. "I assumed we'd keep going around the side of the hill, but it almost looks like we were supposed to go over the top on this one."

"You're right. Let's hope the grade is more gradual on the other side." He looked back up the trail with a frown. "Guess we'd better start taking down markers. It's after three o'clock, and we need to finish before dark."

"Before the barbecue, you mean."

He laughed. "Right. And we sure don't want to lead any riders down here. Come on. We'd better hang extra ribbons up there to make sure." He held out his hand. Ruby took it, and they struggled back up the slope together.

When they finally got back to the Jeep, certain all the markers were placed correctly, it was almost 4:30.

"I don't suppose you'd want to drive back?" Ruby asked, wiping the sleeve of her sweatshirt across her forehead.

"Sure. Are you okay?"

"Yeah, just a little tired."

Chuck put the tools and leftover ribbon in the back of the Jeep. "Well, pile in and let's go get some supper."

Ruby hesitated. "Just a sec."

She walked a few yards to the spot from which they had seen the riders in the ravine. Chuck came to stand beside her. She squinted down into the shadows below and caught her breath.

"Chuck, they're still down there."

"You're right. I can still see the horses. I hope everything's okay. The riders have been gone more than three hours."

"Odd they left those horses tied up that long."

"Oh, wait. It's okay." Chuck pointed off to the left. Just coming into view on the scree from the rockslide were two dark-clad figures.

"That's them," Ruby agreed. "Wonder what they were doing."

"At least we know they're not in trouble," Chuck said. "Probably just exploring. Well, we'd better get going if we don't want to be late for the barbecue."

One of the tiny figures below stopped walking. Ruby caught her breath. The man—she was sure it was a man—was looking up toward where they stood on the ledge. A moment later his companion stopped, too, and turned around. The first person pointed up toward them.

"I think they see us." Ruby raised her arm and waved. There was no response from the hikers. They turned and scrambled over the rest of the rocks to where the horses waited. Within moments the mounted riders disappeared among the spruce trees.

four

Chuck loaded his plate with barbecued ribs, baked beans, and biscuits but made a concession to nutrition by adding a scoop of salad around the edge. He and Ruby found places to sit at one of the tables the crew had set up during their absence along the trail. "What do you want to drink?" he asked. "I'll get it."

"Oh, thanks. Bottled water is fine."

Chuck walked over to the ice-filled coolers that held the drinks and chose spring water for Ruby and a can of cola for himself. He shook the bits of crushed ice from the plastic bottle.

"Hey, Doc," said a voice next to him. He turned and recognized Marcia Bennett, a client whose horse he had treated a few days earlier.

"Hi, Marcia. How's Lady doing?"

"Just fine. She seems to be over that colicky spell."

"Glad to hear it. I'll try to drop by Monday and take a quick look."

"Thanks."

"Are you going to ride tomorrow?" he asked.

"No, I don't do more than five or ten miles at a time. I'm going to help log in riders at checkpoint 3."

"Great. I'm bringing my Appy. It will be our first competitive ride."

"You start out big, Doc."

He grinned. "I just hope I'm not being too ambitious.

We've been training for several months, and the previous owner had him in top condition, so I hope we can last to the finish line."

"Good luck," Marcia said and stooped to pull a can of soda from the cooler.

Chuck hurried back toward the tables. He broke stride for a moment when he spotted Ruby. Seated beside her was a handsome young man about thirty years old and wearing a black Stetson, white shirt, and leather vest. The champ had his eye on Ruby. What was more, Jeff Tavish didn't look as though he'd been working all day. Chuck felt suddenly grubby.

He ambled over and set the water bottle on the table between his plate and Ruby's.

She looked up at him. "Oh, thanks, Chuck. You said you've met Jeff before, right?"

Chuck nodded at the champion. "Hi. Chuck Sullivan." He set down his cola and reached to shake Jeff's outstretched hand.

"Howdy," Jeff said. "I was just giving Ruby some pointers on pacing herself for the 100." He turned his gaze back to Ruby, whose soft brown eyes seemed mesmerized by him. "I'm sure you won't have any trouble finishing, with all the practice rides you tell me you've had, but that first official competition can be stressful. Just relax and enjoy it. That's the main thing."

Ruby's musical chuckle reached Chuck, although she was turned mostly away from him. His view of her glossy brown hair would ordinarily have pleased him, but not when she was chitchatting with another man, especially one who had topnotch horses and had walked away with the trophy two years in a row. Chuck sat down on the bench beside her and brushed away a fly that buzzed around his barbecued ribs. He didn't like the way his appetite had fled because of Jeff's proximity. Last year he'd cheered him on and congratulated him on his win. What right did he have to treat him differently now?

"So you've entered the ride? What kind of horse have you got?"

Chuck realized Jeff was addressing him. He leaned forward to look past Ruby. "Oh, uh, Appaloosa gelding."

"Yeah?"

Ruby said, "Rascal's a terrific horse. I know he'll do well tomorrow. We had a forty-mile trail ride last weekend, and he came through it like a pro."

Jeff nodded and looked from her to Chuck and back. The brim of the Stetson shaded Jeff's eyes, but Chuck thought he detected a bit of speculation going on.

"So what did you all do today?" Jeff asked.

Chuck let Ruby tell him about their trek along the old stagecoach road while he dove into his cooling food.

"It's gorgeous up there. Panoramic views at every turn."

"I can't wait to see that part of the trail." Jeff's eyes glistened. "I love riding new ground, although it probably means I won't shorten my time any, having to go over terrain I don't know. But it's fun."

"Yes, it's a beautiful area," Ruby said. "There are some places where you have to be careful, though. Sheer drop-offs and steep grades."

"On the stagecoach route?" Jeff popped the top on a can of root beer.

"Well, the worst part we saw wasn't actually on the route for tomorrow's ride," Ruby admitted, "but there are a couple of spots where you don't want to get too close to the edge."

Jeff tipped up his can and took a deep swallow.

"I was surprised to learn they took coaches through these mountains," Chuck said.

"Well, back in the mining heyday they cut some pretty precarious roads." Jeff picked up his fork and looked at them eagerly. "Hey, did you hear about the payroll robbery?"

Ruby shook her head. "I usually hear about all the crime in these parts."

"Oh, this was a long time ago," Jeff said. "Back in the 1880s, I think. They say a stagecoach carrying a payroll was robbed somewhere in these parts. The robbers drove off in the coach, leaving the driver dead and the passengers tied up. The marshal got up a posse to chase the thieves, but the stagecoach was never found."

"I think I've heard something about that before," Ruby said.

Jeff nodded and picked up a biscuit. "Some people think the coach wrecked in these mountains and the money is still out there somewhere."

"Doubt it," Chuck said. "That's a long, long time ago. Somebody would have found it by now." He thought of the hikers they'd seen that day, poking around in the ravine. There probably wasn't a square foot of land in Wyoming nobody had walked over in the last hundred and twenty years.

"Not necessarily." Jeff lowered his voice to a spectral tone. "Some folks say the coach still roams these hills, with a ghostly driver holding the reins."

Ruby shivered. "I don't believe in ghosts."

Jeff laughed. "Me either, but it makes a good story."

They continued to talk, with Jeff carrying most of the conversation. Allison and Marcia sat down across the table from them.

"We've got a record number of entries for the ride to-morrow," Allison told them with a proud smile.

"How many?" Ruby asked.

"Sixty-eight."

"Wow! That's a lot."

"It will take us longer to check everyone in. I hope folks get over to the registration booth early," Allison said. "Of course, most of them did their preliminary vet checks this afternoon."

"We're planning to get ours done in the morning," Chuck said, sliding a glance at Ruby.

"Well, be here by five," Allison said. "I doubt we can get another vet here any earlier to check you in."

They continued to talk about the competition. The sun sank behind the trees, and Tom Marden put a match to the pile of wood the volunteers had prepared for a bonfire. Chuck noticed Ruby rubbed her arms as if to warm them.

"I don't want to rush your eating, folks," Tom called, "but gather round the fire when you're done. We'll go over the particulars for the ride. You should have picked up a packet with your maps and other information, but we'll review a few things. And for afterward Dick and Rory brought their guitars. Let's sing a few cowboy songs. What do you say?"

The crowd began to drift toward the fireside.

"Last call on beans and barbecue," Loreta Halstead called.

"Oops, that's my cue," Jeff said, rising. "I've been gabbing so much I almost missed out on seconds."

Chuck wasn't sorry to see him go. He leaned closer to Ruby. "Are you finished?"

"Yes, I'm stuffed. But you get some dessert if you want it."

"No, I'm fine."

"Well, I'm getting some," Allison said. She and Marcia

went in search of the dessert table.

"You sure?" Chuck asked. He saw Jeff heading back toward them carrying his newly heaped plate. "We can go over to the fire if you want."

Ruby stood and gathered up their plastic silverware, paper plates, and napkins. Chuck took the drink containers, and they made a stop at the cleanup area. People were opening canvas chairs or spreading throws on the ground near the fire.

"We should have brought something to sit on," Chuck noted.

"Oh, I've got Lancelot's old blanket in the back of the Jeep," Ruby said.

They were soon settled cozily among the laughing horsemen. For the next half hour Tom Marden and Allison Bowie reviewed safety concerns, unique features of the trail, and procedures at checkpoints. Jeff Tavish stood at the edge of the crowd with a couple of other men. When all questions had been answered, Tom called on the two musicians.

Dick Halstead strummed his guitar and started singing "Riding Home." Those who knew the old song joined in. As the shadows deepened, Chuck found himself watching the firelight play on Ruby's face. He was sitting next to the prettiest woman at the gathering. Her hair glistened a deep chestnut in the firelight. She glanced over at him and smiled, and Chuck's heart flipped.

"Excuse me. Got room for one more?" Jeff sank down on Ruby's other side and crossed his long legs, his cowboy boots sticking out between two other people toward the fire.

"Sure, Jeff." Ruby edged over a little closer to Chuck, and he told himself this wasn't a bad thing. Ruby's shoulder touched his sleeve now. He didn't mind a bit. He tried not to think about Jeff. They were all adults, and he had no reason to be jealous. Ruby had chosen to spend the day with him. She could have invited Jeff to help them hang trail markers, but she didn't. And Jeff had inserted himself into their suppertime, he was sure, just as he did now at the campfire.

After a few more songs Tom told how the Medicine Bow Mountains acquired their name.

"The Indians used to cut the cedars to make their bows. The wood was tough and springy, and it made such great bows they thought it was good medicine to use that wood."

"That's a great story, Tom," Hester said.

"Hey, I've got a story," Jeff called. "It's about the haunted stagecoach. Ever hear it?"

Ruby leaned close to Chuck. "Not again."

"Oh, well," Chuck said. Ruby smiled at him, and that made listening to Jeff's tale again tolerable.

Jeff's voice rose and fell, and he leaned forward with a sweep of his hand as he told of the stagecoach robbery. The crowd listened intently, and Jeff's story sprouted new details. "And those people swore afterward they could see right through the robbers."

Ruby scrunched up her face and shot Chuck an inquiring look as she listened to the latest embellishments.

"And those robbers stole all the people's jewelry and money, and they climbed up on the stagecoach and drove off with it and the payroll. A coach with a six-horse hitch and two transparent robbers. It drove off up the trail where we're going to ride tomorrow, and the folks hereabouts never saw that coach again."

"That's quite a story, Jeff," Allison said. "I've never heard it told quite that way."

"Kinda spooky," Dick said.

"That's not all," Jeff shot back. "Folks say if you're up there on the mountain at midnight on a full moon evening, you might see the coach roll by with those two robbers on the seat, and if you look just right you'll see the moonlight shine right through 'em."

"Folks *say*." Hester Marden's tone was laced with sarcasm.

"Well, *Jeff* says, anyway," her husband, Tom, retorted. The crowd laughed, and Tom said, "Hey, Rory, Dick, how about another tune?"

Jeff called out, "Yeah, how about 'Ghost Riders in the Sky'?"

Chuck knew it was all in fun, but as the eerie melody echoed around them he noticed Ruby's face was sober. He leaned over and whispered, "You all right?"

She nodded. "I'm tired, though. Guess I should head home soon."

"We can leave anytime," Chuck told her.

She seemed to consider, and as the song ended she nodded and stirred. "Excuse me, Jeff. I hate to take your sitting place away, but I'll need the blanket."

"What—you're leaving?"

Ruby nodded. "Yeah, it's time for me to hit the road."

"You're not scared, are you?" Jeff stood and scooped up the blanket for her. "I can give you a lift home if you don't want to drive alone."

She chuckled. "That's okay. I'm fine. But we have a long day ahead of us tomorrow."

Chuck reached out and took the wadded blanket from Jeff's hands. "Thanks, Jeff. We'll see you in the morning."

He was rewarded by a chagrined look from the champ. Chuck wished he'd arranged to pick Ruby up that morning and drive her home. He walked beside her to the Jeep and stowed the blanket for her.

"You sure you'll be okay?" he asked.

"Absolutely. Are you heading out now, too, or are you going to stay awhile longer?"

Chuck didn't even glance back toward the fire. "I'm going. I can follow you as far as the turnoff for your road."

She smiled. "Thanks. Hey, isn't that a full moon up there? I wonder if the old stagecoach will ride tonight."

Chuck laughed. "You're a good sport."

"Well, I've got to admit that when Jeff told that story I was thinking of the riders we saw today."

"Oh? I wondered about them, too."

"It was probably nothing," Ruby said.

Chuck opened the Jeep door for her. "Well, drive safely. I'll see you in about ten hours." He reached out and gave her hand a squeeze. Ruby's smile caught the moonlight with a dazzling gleam. Chuck's social life was definitely on the upswing. He left her and went to his pickup, already thinking about seeing her again tomorrow. But as soon as he arrived home he pulled out his detailed topographical maps of the ride area and searched them for a trail in the location where they had seen the horses.

five

Ruby paced her room in her pajamas, too keyed up to sleep. Memories of the day played over and over in her mind—her time with Chuck, Jeff's attention to her, the mysterious riders in the ravine. She knew she needed to rest so she would be at her best tomorrow. She owed it to Lancelot.

She paced to the window, her bare toes scooting across the carpet. Pushing the curtain aside, she peered out toward the barn. Everything lay still and peaceful, but she couldn't help imagining the ghostly stagecoach tearing up her parents' driveway.

With a sigh she scuffed back to the bed and sat down. The clock on her night table told her it was nearly eleven o'clock.

Would Chuck want to ride with her tomorrow? In these competitions it was every man for himself if that man wanted to win; she knew that. You couldn't loll around waiting for your friends and hope to make the top ten.

Rascal was a good horse, and Chuck rode well enough to place in the ride, even though he was inexperienced in the sport. Chances were they wouldn't have consecutive numbers, in which case they wouldn't start near each other. The race had a staggered start, with riders leaving the holding area two minutes apart. She might not see Chuck and Rascal all day. And if they did start close together she would tell him to go on without her. Especially if Lancelot wasn't keeping up with Rascal, though they were both in top condition and had seemed evenly matched on their practice ride.

She picked up the pewter frame she kept beside her bed. She and her sister, Julie, peered out at her, laughing and carefree. *I miss you so much!* What wouldn't she give to have Julie at the ride with her tomorrow?

Ruby closed her eyes in prayer. *Lord, thank You for this opportunity. I just want a fun, safe day, that's all. I don't want to get all caught up in thinking about Chuck. Let me concentrate on the ride. I don't ask You to let me finish in the top ten. I just want to make it through in the twenty-four-hour time limit, with Lancelot in good condition. And as for Chuck. . .well, yeah, I like him. A lot. But if he's not the one You have in mind for me, then help me not to get too carried away in thinking about him.*

She replaced the frame on the nightstand and climbed into bed. After reading a psalm she turned off the lamp and went over the ride route in her mind. Maybe she should have camped at the tenting area down the road from the ride start like the others. She could have trailered Lancelot over today and taken care of the pre-ride veterinary exam. She hoped her palomino was getting more rest than she was. The moonlight streamed in between her eyelet curtains. Ruby rolled over and closed her eyes.

When she woke again, her luminous clock said 3:30. The ride was scheduled to start at six, and Allison had suggested arriving an hour early. Probably most of the riders would arrive at the starting area around five. Ruby slipped out of bed and pulled on her clothes. Tiptoeing down the stairs with her shoes in her hand so she wouldn't wake her parents, she determined to force down breakfast, even though she didn't feel like it. While her bagel toasted she checked over her pile of gear on the table. Canteen, water bottle, hat, sweatshirt, hoof pick, granola bars.

"Figured you'd be up early."

She jumped and turned to face her father, who leaned against the kitchen doorjamb.

"Hi, Dad. I hope I didn't wake you up."

"I don't know if you did or not, but how about a cup of coffee?"

She grinned. "Sure. I'll put some on. Want a bagel with it?"

"Why not?" He opened the refrigerator while she measured the coffee grounds. By the time the coffee began brewing and the first bagels had toasted, he'd lined up margarine, jam, cream cheese, and honey.

"Wow. Quite a spread," she said dubiously.

"Nothing like a pre-dawn bagel party." He opened a drawer and selected knives and spoons.

Ruby checked the sugar bowl to make sure it wasn't empty. Her father took a teaspoon in each cup of coffee. They sat down together, and Dad asked a blessing, seeking special care and safety for all the riders.

The coffee was only half brewed. Ruby held a mug next to the machine and quickly yanked the carafe out, slipping the mug beneath the flowing stream of coffee. Although she was quick, a couple of drops splashed on the hot base and sizzled.

She slid the carafe back in place and carried the full mug to the table. "Here you go, Dad."

"Thanks. Are you nervous?"

"A little."

"Well, we'll be there with the lunch basket, waiting for you at Eight-Mile Creek."

"Thanks. I wish you could see the race, but there's no good place where you can watch much of it."

"Don't worry about it. What's the earliest you could get to the checkpoint?" Her father sipped his coffee and set the mug down.

"I hope to be there by noon, but it could be one or later if things don't go well."

"We'll be there at eleven in case you're early. But don't worry if you're late. We'll enjoy the scenery and cheer on the riders that come in ahead of you. We'll be praying for you, too."

"Thanks. The first part of the ride is the easiest, so I have hopes of getting to the lunch stop by noon. It's forty miles on the trail."

"Really? I think it's less than twenty miles from here. You know, Grandma said she and Elsie will come. I told her they can't take their semitruck on the mountain road, so they're coming to the house and will ride up there with us."

"Oh, that will be neat." Ruby smiled just thinking about the pink semi with gold lettering that her grandmother and her sister-in-law, Elsie Daniels, roamed the roads in. The two widows hauled limited amounts of freight for businesses their husbands worked with in the old days and loved their adventures on the road. "When are they going to retire, anyway?"

"When they're good and ready, I guess. Believe me, I've tried to talk them into it. Your cousin Dylan may be coming, too, and maybe Holly." Dad spread cream cheese on his half of the first bagel and topped it with a squirt of honey.

Ruby poured orange juice for herself and put a little cream cheese and strawberry jam on her half of the bagel. Behind her on the counter, the second one popped up in the toaster.

"I'll get it." Dad jumped up and grabbed the hot bagel halves, dropping them onto his plate. "Ouch. Hey, where did you get cranberry bagels?"

"Not me. Mom must have found them somewhere." Ruby accepted one and decided to eat it plain while it was hot. "Yum. You were right, Dad. This is fun. Thanks. Like I said, I'm a little nervous."

"You'll do great." He took a bite of the cranberry bagel, slathered in cream cheese, and closed his eyes. "Mm. That's even better than the cheese and tomato bagels." He chewed another bite and swallowed. "So, honey, we'll all be over at the finish line to see you come in at the end of the ride tonight."

"That's fantastic, Dad. Thank you." She wiped her hands, stood, and reached for her sweatshirt.

"Want me to help you load Lancelot?" he asked.

"No, I'll be fine. I packed his tack in the trailer last night."

"Well, I already hitched the trailer to the truck for you."

"Great. I'll see you later, Dad." She stooped to kiss his cheek and went out into the dark, damp morning. When she opened the stable door, Lancelot nickered softly.

"Good morning, fella."

She walked to his stall door and stroked his nose then scratched around his ears. Lancelot whuffed in response and rubbed his head against her shoulder. Ruby brought him a short ration of oats and a bucket of water. As he ate, she went over his glistening golden coat with a soft brush.

"We're going to have fun today," she told him. His soft whicker made her smile.

At 4:15 a.m. she led Lancelot out to the horse trailer, and he stepped eagerly up the ramp. Ruby hooked the cross ties to his halter and gave his withers a final pat. The drive to the starting area was only a few miles, and she knew she'd be very early, but she didn't mind. She and Lancelot could enjoy the dawn and watch the other competitors arrive.

She passed the road to the campground but didn't see any vehicles coming out. When she came to the gravel road leading to the field where the race would start, she flipped on her turn signal. Just as she was about to swing onto the road, a light-colored pickup truck emerged. Ruby eyed it in surprise. She wasn't the earliest of the early birds, after all. The driver pulled out onto the paved road without making eye contact. He seemed to be in a hurry. She didn't recognize him, but stocky men in Stetsons were a dime a dozen in Wyoming.

She eased her rig carefully onto the smaller road and drove slowly toward the field. A whiff of smoke caught her attention. Last night's bonfire was held at the campground. Surely she wouldn't be able to smell any lingering hints of it from here. The field used as a parking area opened before her. The unnatural glow in the early dawn pulled her gaze toward the registration booth, and she almost jammed on the brakes but squeezed the pedal down slowly out of deference to Lancelot. The wooden booth was engulfed in flames.

six

Ruby pulled out her cell phone with trembling hands and keyed 911.

"This is Ruby Dale. There's a structure fire off the Howard Road at the field where the endurance ride is supposed to start this morning. It's on the Landry ranch." She gave the dispatcher her cell phone number and more precise directions.

The fire crackled, and inside the trailer Lancelot pawed and whinnied. As the wooden booth crumpled and collapsed, embers fell to the ground. The dry grass surrounding it flared up in several spots. Ruby was torn by the desire to run over and try to stamp out the smaller fires, but Lancelot's safety came first. She threw the truck into gear and drove out to the paved road. She pulled to the side and opened her door. In a matter of minutes a siren greeted her ears. The small town fire department's obsessive drilling had paid off with a quick response time.

The first fire truck roared down the road but slowed as it neared her. The driver brought it to a stop beside her and killed the siren. Ruby squinted against the flashing red lights and pointed up the gravel road.

"Up there in the field," she called, pointing.

The ladder truck swung onto the side road, and a stream of cars and pickup trucks followed, some pulling horse trailers. Ruby drove slowly down the road to a place where she could safely turn her rig around and then went back to the field.

A second fire truck—a pumper with a large tank body—swooped past her.

By the time she returned to the starting area, dawn had broken over the plains. The fire was out. Competitors, volunteers, and ride officials gathered in clusters to stare at the firemen as they rolled their hoses.

As she climbed down from the truck, Chuck approached and called out to her.

"Ruby! You missed the excitement."

She gave him a shaky smile. "Hi, Chuck. Actually I think I was here at the start of it." She told him what she had found on her arrival, and he whistled.

"You should talk to the fire chief. He was asking if anyone knew who called 911."

One crew of firefighters was still soaking the grass in a wide swath around where the blaze had been. Chuck pointed toward them.

"The chief's over there."

Ruby nodded and swallowed. Her throat felt scratchy. "Okay."

Chuck took her hand. "Come on. I'll go with you."

She smiled up at him. "Thanks. This wasn't exactly how I envisioned the start of this day."

Chief Ripton greeted her soberly then stepped aside with her and Chuck and listened to her explanation.

"It's a good thing you came along early, Miss Dale, and that you had a cell phone. If the grass fire had spread, this whole area could have gone up in flames."

Ruby gulped. "In that case I'm glad I was too nervous to sleep late."

"How far advanced was the fire when you first saw it?" Ripton asked.

She shuddered, recalling that first moment of realization. "It was. . .the booth was already burning. Flames were all over the counter area and running up the roof supports."

The chief nodded. "What else did you see?"

"I. . ." She glanced toward Chuck. For the first time she realized he was still holding her hand. "I saw a truck pull out of here when I came. A pickup. A. . .maybe a Dodge, I'm not sure. But it was a full-sized pickup, and it was light. Gray or tan maybe. I don't think it was white, but the sun wasn't up then."

The chief produced a notebook from somewhere within his turnout gear. "I want to take your name and contact information, in case the fire marshal wants to talk to you later."

"Sure," Ruby said.

Chuck squeezed her hand. "She's entered in the ride," he told the chief. "She'll be on the trail all day."

"I wish you success," Ripton said. Ruby gave him the data he requested, and he wrote it down. "Miss Dale, did you get a look at the driver of that truck?"

She squeezed her eyes shut. Her knees felt a little wobbly, and she was glad Chuck was beside her. She clung to his hand shamelessly and opened her eyes to face the chief.

"He was wearing a cowboy hat, low over his eyes, but I had the impression of a big man. Stocky. He was white. No beard or glasses. His. . .his chin. . ." She thought hard about what she had seen. "His jaw was kind of square. He didn't really look at me, and he peeled out onto the road as though he was in a big hurry."

"No doubt," Ripton said dryly. "Anything else?"

She hesitated, trying to recall every detail. "He had something hanging from the rearview mirror. Not those stupid dice, but something. Maybe an air freshener." She shrugged. "I'm sorry. That's about all I can remember."

"You're doing great," Chuck murmured, and a pleasant warmth slid through her.

The chief tucked his notebook away. "Thank you very much, Miss Dale. I hope you do well in the ride, and we'll be in touch later. This was definitely arson."

☙

Chuck led Ruby back toward her rig. She staggered suddenly, and he slid his arm around her waist.

"Are you okay?"

"Yes. Sorry. My legs are a little rubbery."

He tightened his grip on her. "Let's just take it easy then. This was a bit of a shock, wasn't it?"

They approached her pickup, and he could hear Lancelot pawing inside the horse trailer. The smell of smoke still hung in the air.

"How about if you sit down for a minute and I get Lancelot out of the trailer?" Chuck asked.

"Yes, the poor thing." She glanced up at him with wide eyes. "Thank you. They will hold the ride, won't they? I mean, this won't stop it?"

"Oh, I don't think so." He glanced at his watch and noted it was already the starting time and he'd done no preparation beyond getting Rascal out of his trailer. He looked around the field for signs of activity among the ride officials. "Look over there." He pointed to where Tom Marden and Allison Bowie were setting up a folding table. "I think they're going to make do and keep things rolling."

"That's good." Ruby's voice held only a slight tremor now. "I haven't done my vet check."

"Me either. Just sit for a minute, and as soon as I get your horse on the ground we'll find out what they're planning."

Ruby opened the driver's door of her dad's truck and climbed in, leaving the door open. Chuck went to the back of her trailer and lowered the ramp. Lancelot whinnied. Chuck walked up the ramp, speaking softly to the palomino. As soon as he'd unsnapped the cross ties, Lancelot backed up and found his footing on the ramp. His steps thudded loudly as they edged to the ground. Chuck hitched the horse to the bracket on the side of the trailer and stroked his glossy neck, speaking gently to him. Other riders and spectators had arrived by the scheduled start time, crowding the parking area. People walked by leading horses and carrying buckets and tack. Chuck nodded to those who called greetings as he walked over to where Ruby sat. He leaned down, bracing against the doorframe.

"How are you doing?"

"Good," she said. "Thanks again."

"You're welcome. You know, I've been thinking about the fire and all."

"And?"

He watched her sober face. "God must have a reason for allowing this to happen."

Ruby managed a shaky smile. "That's just what I was thinking. The arson seems meaningless and cruel, but we don't know what God has planned. I was sitting here thanking Him for bringing me out early and helping the firefighters stop it so quickly. God is in control here, for sure."

Chuck reached out and squeezed her shoulder. "I'm glad you're thinking that way."

"Hey, Doc!"

Chuck looked up to see Jeff Tavish walking toward them. He straightened. "Morning, Jeff."

Jeff wore a bright red Western shirt trimmed in black and

a cream-colored Stetson with soft, worn jeans. Chuck looked closely at his footwear and noted that, though they gleamed, Jeff's black cowboy boots had seen a lot of wear. No doubt the champion would be comfortable today, but he would still cut a dashing figure for cameras at the finish line.

"I got here after the excitement," Jeff said, "but Tom Marden told me Ruby's the heroine of the day."

Chuck smiled, but a glance at Ruby told him she was uneasy with the designation. She climbed out of the truck cab and stood beside him.

"I just got here before anyone else, that's all. One of the blessings of insomnia."

"You're too modest," Jeff said. "They told me your quick action kept the fire from spreading. This could have been a disaster if it got away and started burning range land."

Tom Marden's booming voice, made even louder with a bullhorn, called out, "Attention, everyone! The ride officials have decided the ride will go forward, but the start will be delayed sixty minutes. The first riders will leave the gate at seven o'clock, which is just over a half hour from now."

All over the field, riders let out a cheer.

"Of course, the maximum finish time will also be adjusted to 7:00 a.m. tomorrow," Tom went on. "Our ride secretary is now set up to register the competitors, and the judges have a special request. They would like Miss Ruby Dale to come to the registration table where the ride secretary will present her with bib number 1, in recognition of her role in stopping the fire this morning."

Ruby's face went scarlet, and she looked up at Chuck. He smiled, thinking how attractive her modesty made her. He grinned at her and jerked his head toward the registration table. "Come on. Let's get you over there so we don't hold things up any longer."

He and Jeff walked on either side of Ruby as she crossed the parking area to resounding cheers and applause. She raised her hand in a shy wave and lowered her gaze as soon as she reached the table. Allison Bowie handed her a numbered bib.

"Let's see, Ruby. You haven't had your vet check yet."

"I know. Is there time? Chuck's horse hasn't been vetted either."

Allison pointed across the field. "Dr. Hogan and Dr. Sawtelle are over there right now. Better hustle."

"Thanks." Ruby looked at Chuck.

"Go ahead," he said. "I'll be right behind you."

"Okay, thanks." She threw a smile in Jeff's general direction and hurried toward her rig.

Jeff stood back and gestured for Chuck to go next. Chuck nodded and smiled at him and quickly gave Allison his information. She handed him bib number 2. Hester Marden had begun registering more riders at the other end of the table, and he saw Jeff had number 3. Chuck would just as soon Jeff was farther down the line of riders. *Oh, well, if he passes us first thing, we won't have to worry about him for the rest of the day.*

He realized he was jealous of the champion, and not because of Jeff's riding ability or his flashy good looks. Chuck sent up a quick prayer for calmness and God's guidance as he saddled Rascal.

When both their horses had passed the veterinarians' inspection, Ruby walked over to his truck, leading Lancelot. The palomino tossed his head and nickered. Rascal pulled his head around, stretching the tie rope taut, to look at his friend and whinny in response.

"I think these two are buddies for life," Ruby said with a chuckle.

"That's good. Horses need social interaction just like people."

"Is someone meeting you at the noon stop?" She hitched Lancelot to the side of the trailer.

"Just Dr. Hogan. As soon as all the riders have started, he'll drive up there. He's manning the vet check at the lunch stop today, and he has a ration and a water bucket for Rascal in his car."

"My folks are coming."

"Great."

Ruby had braided her hair, he noted. Although she seemed calm now, her face was still pale.

"I've got some cold drinks in my cooler," he said. "Would you like some juice?"

"That sounds good. But you need to finish getting Rascal ready. Anything I can do to help?"

"No, I'm all set except for putting this bib on. Why don't you help yourself and bring me a bottle of apple juice?"

"Okay." Her dark braid hung down below her hat against the back of her blue gingham-checked shirt as she leaned over the side of his truck's bed and opened the cooler.

Chuck tore his gaze away and pulled the marked bib over his head. *I'm riding in back of the prettiest cowgirl in Wyoming,* he thought. *If I have to eat Ruby's dust all day, at least I'll have a terrific view.*

As he tied the strings to anchor his bib, Ruby returned with two bottles. Chuck stowed Rascal's halter and lead rope in his saddlebag and took the bottle of juice she held out.

"Hey, how you folks doing?" Jeff Tavish led his horse over close to them. Chuck looked over the compact bay mare with appreciation. Close coupled with a deep chest, she looked wiry and tough. No doubt she had the stamina to complete the rugged ride.

"Is this the horse you won on last year?" Chuck asked.

"Sure is. Her name is Annabelle." Jeff beamed with pride and stroked his mare's shoulder.

"She has to be the best endurance horse ever." Ruby's eyes practically glowed as she gazed at Annabelle.

"Thanks. What's you all's strategy?" Jeff might be addressing them both, but he looked only at Ruby.

"I'm not sure I have one," Chuck said. "I just want to finish safely."

Ruby smiled at him. "Me, too, but I was figuring to start out with a canter across the fields. We'll have plenty of slow places when we get up in the hills."

Jeff nodded. "Yeah, that's good. But you want to keep your time down if you can. Remember—it's not the horse that crosses the finish line first; it's the one with the shortest overall ride time. So you can leave first and finish first, but if Chuck finishes a minute after you do he's the winner, since he's starting two minutes later."

She nodded and shot a glance at Chuck. "Well, I'll keep an eye on this hombre if he starts creeping up on me."

They all chuckled, and Jeff asked, "Do you want to stick together for the first leg?"

Chuck eyed him in surprise. He'd figured the champ would breeze past them and lead the entire race. "Is that what you usually do?"

Jeff shrugged. "Sometimes. It's good to have a buddy or two at the start. It's not like a short race. Pacing is critical. These horses need some energy left for the second half, so I like to start out at a moderate pace and enjoy it."

Ruby smiled at Chuck. "It might be fun to ride together for a while. But if you guys find I'm slowing you down you need to go on ahead and not worry about Lancelot and me."

"You'll probably do better than me," Chuck said with a shrug.

"We'll stay together if it works for us then," Jeff said. "If it's holding anyone back, then it's every man for himself. Or woman."

Ruby grinned. "Got it. Do you want me to start out slower—just trot along?"

"No need," Jeff said. "We'll catch up. Right, Chuck?"

"Sure." Chuck wondered if he'd just agreed to an alliance that would cost him Ruby's attentions as well as a chance to lead the pack for a while. Once Jeff caught up to him and Ruby, there would be no question of who the ultimate winner would be. And as far as Ruby's heart was concerned. . .he eyed her as she chatted with Jeff. Her smile for the champ was as bright as the one she'd bestowed on Chuck earlier.

"Attention," came Tom's unignorable voice. "The ride will begin in five minutes. Will the first riders please report to the starting line? Number one is Ruby Dale, riding Lancelot. On deck is Dr. Chuck Sullivan on Rascal."

Ruby took a quick sip from her bottle. Her hands quivered a little as she replaced the cover. "Guess we need to look sharp."

"I'll put that away for you." Chuck took the bottle and placed it with his in the cooler. When he turned around again, Ruby had mounted and was gathering her reins.

"So we'll stick together at least until the checkpoint at Mile 10," Jeff said, grinning up at her.

"Got it." Ruby took a deep breath and looked over at Chuck. "Are you ready?"

"Yep, I'm right behind you." Chuck reached for Rascal's reins.

As Ruby trotted Lancelot toward the starting box, Jeff

stepped closer to Chuck and extended his right hand. "Well, Doc, I wish you luck."

Chuck smiled and shook his hand. "May the best man and horse win."

Jeff grinned. "Oh, I think you've already won."

Chuck stared after him as Jeff turned and led Annabelle away.

seven

Ruby waited just outside the starting box. Chuck had mounted and was riding her way. He and Rascal reached her just as Tom Marden called, "Two minutes to start."

"Time for you and Lancelot to get into the starting box." Chuck nodded toward the area marked out on the grass with lines of flour.

Ruby glanced toward the officials' table. "I was wondering if we had time to pray."

Chuck's smile melted away any lingering nervousness.

"Sure." He sidled Rascal up next to Lancelot, and the Appaloosa snuffled Lancelot's face. "We'll have to keep it short." Chuck bowed his head, and Ruby followed suit. "Lord, we thank You for bringing us here for this exciting day in such a beautiful setting. We ask that You'd give us a good time today and, above all, safety. Amen."

"Amen," Ruby said and opened her eyes. Chuck's blue eyes regarded her soberly.

"Better get in the box," he said. "I'll see you soon, if you don't decide to gallop off in a cloud of dust."

She smiled. "You don't have to worry about that."

"One minute to go," said Tom Marden.

Lancelot seemed reluctant to leave Rascal but obeyed when Ruby pressed his side with her leg. He pivoted and entered the rectangle marked on the dry grass. She fingered her bib to make sure it lay flat against her shirt and pushed her hat back a bit. She'd considered wearing a more fashionable

Stetson today but had opted for her comfortable old baseball cap. The sun had risen above the horizon and promised them a clear, warm day. She patted the pack behind her saddle's cantle. Canteen, sweatshirt, granola bars, trail map. Check. She could almost feel the stares of the spectators and the sixty-seven other contestants. When she glanced back at Chuck he raised his hand to his hat brim in salute, and she felt a surge of adrenaline.

"Rider number 1, go," came Tom's voice. He continued talking as she urged Lancelot forward. "Folks, the Wyoming 100 has officially opened, with Ruby Dale and Lancelot riding out first. Rider number 2 will enter the starting box. That's Dr. Chuck Sullivan on Rascal. On deck is number 3, Jeff Tavish, our current champion, riding Annabelle."

Tom's voice faded as Ruby set off along the edge of the field to where the trail skirted a fenced pasture, crossed a creek, and continued fairly flat for a half mile along a Jeep road. Her slight trepidation kept her on edge. *This is it,* she told herself. She leaned forward and patted Lancelot's withers. "Okay, fella, this is what we've trained for. Let's go."

She squeezed him with her legs and gave him plenty of rein. Lancelot slipped into his easy canter. Ruby grinned as they flew along the verge of the field. For two glorious minutes they were alone on the course, setting the pace for all those behind. She was glad she knew the route well.

To her right the wire fence bounded the trail, and a herd of Hereford cattle grazed in the pasture. For the most part they ignored her, but a steer near the edge of the enclosure lifted its head and watched her and Lancelot fly past. It let out a mournful lowing, and Ruby laughed as they approached a rustic wooden bridge. The rancher maintained the span over a small stream that flowed through his property. The sturdy structure was held up by stone abutments on each end. They slowed to a trot, and Lancelot's shod hooves struck the decking made of two-by-eight boards. His hoofbeats echoed, but he reacted only with a twitch of his ears.

"Good boy," Ruby said as he stepped evenly forward over the bridge. She was now on a gravel road the rancher used to access the back acres of his land. Looking over her shoulder, she realized they were out of sight of the starting area. It felt a little strange to be out here in front, all alone. Again she thought of Julie. They'd done everything together, it seemed, until they were separated by death. Julie would have loved this ride. "I love you, Jules," she whispered. Could her sister see her now?

Lancelot lowered his head and quickened his steps. Ruby let him slip back into a canter. They approached a stand of rather spindly spruce trees. She looked back toward the bridge again. No sign of Chuck yet. As Lancelot loped along, she wondered if she should slow down. No, the two men had told her to set her own pace. Lancelot was fresh. She couldn't see any sense in wasting time on this easy stretch. Plenty of time for a slower gait later on.

The sun filtered through the tree branches as she followed the trail through the sparse woods. A sudden flash of movement ahead startled her, and Lancelot flinched as a deer bounded across the trail, but he continued steadily onward. She came to a spot where three ribbon markers indicated a turn onto a narrower path that eased upward into the foothills. As she turned Lancelot onto it, she heard hoofbeats behind her.

A glance over her shoulder told her Chuck and Rascal were fast closing the gap between them. She fought the instinct to stop and wait for them but let Lancelot trot up the slight incline. The smell of the evergreens and the sounds of creaking leather and hooves on the trail engulfed her.

She looked back again. Chuck waved. He might have been riding a solid brown horse from what she could see of Rascal. The gelding's dark head, shoulders, and legs, with only a strip of white on his nose, gave no hint of his glorious white markings behind the saddle.

"The trail widens out ahead," Ruby called as Chuck brought his mount up closer. "Want to canter a while longer?"

"Sure," he replied. "Let's make all the time we can without tiring them out."

She turned forward, urging Lancelot to resume his canter. He snorted and picked up the pace, running easily along the gently undulating trail. A short distance later they emerged onto an almost flat meadow owned by the Bureau of Land Management. Most of the grassy area was fenced by an abutting rancher, but there was plenty of space along the edge for the two horses to run side by side. As Rascal overtook Lancelot, Ruby looked at Chuck. His grin of sheer delight made her laugh. Something about racing across country on an eager horse inspired a confident joy deep inside her.

At the far side of the meadow the grassy trail again wove through a scanty copse. Chuck slowed Rascal to allow Ruby to move her horse ahead of his.

"Jeff's coming up," he said, and Ruby looked back.

The bay Arabian mare tore along the trail at the edge of the meadow, her black mane floating in the breeze of her speed. Ruby could spot Jeff a mile away with his light-colored hat and blazing red shirt.

"Think she's going flat out?" she asked.

Chuck shook his head. "Naw, she's just stretching her legs. I'll bet she could do a lot faster on a racetrack."

Ruby realized they'd slowed to a walk. She clucked to Lancelot, squeezing his sides. Might as well let Jeff work a little to catch up to them.

❧

Jeff's bay mare galloped up fast behind Chuck. Rascal snorted and flicked his ears back and forth. The rhythm of Annabelle's hoofbeats changed, and the mare whinnied.

Chuck looked back and waved at Jeff. The path was too narrow for them to ride abreast, so Annabelle fell in behind them.

Ruby slowed her mount as they approached a downward sloping bank, and Chuck pulled Rascal down to a trot. Ruby pushed Lancelot forward. The palomino bounded down the bank and picked up a gravel road around the edge of a large hayfield.

Chuck gave Rascal an encouraging nudge, and the Appaloosa followed Lancelot without hesitation. Almost as soon as they hit the gravel road, Annabelle galloped past and fell into stride with Ruby's horse.

"Ready to move out?" Jeff yelled.

Ruby threw a questioning look over her shoulder at Chuck. Part of him wanted to say, "No, you go on ahead." Wouldn't a leisurely ride with Ruby be better than maintaining their lead on the pack that would follow? The other part of him wanted to behave like a serious contender and give himself every advantage he could. What sense did it make to enter a competitive ride and not act like a competitor?

Was the alliance a mistake? Jeff had agreed that if he felt they held him back he'd move out alone, but he'd also agreed to keep the threesome intact until the first checkpoint. Chuck had thought Rascal moved quickly, but compared to Annabelle his mount was a plodder. Maybe the defending champion would tire of waiting for them and leave them well before Mile 10.

They went on steadily, trotting most of the time, cantering on open stretches and walking on steeper grades, but Chuck knew they were still in the easy part. Just after Mile 5 they picked their way downhill to a swift-flowing stream. When Ruby and Chuck caught up to Jeff, he had dismounted and led Annabelle down to the water so she could drink.

"How you folks doing?" Jeff called.

"Fine," Ruby said. "We're going a little faster than I usually do."

"We'll have to slow down now. The trail gets a lot more rugged after this." Annabelle raised her head and shook it, splattering Jeff with water droplets. He led her up the bank and out of the way.

Ruby led Lancelot down to the edge of the stream.

Jeff turned his horse in a circle so that he stood near Chuck. "Do we need to take it easier?"

Chuck shrugged. "You're the pro, Jeff. Ruby and I probably aren't used to pushing hard at the start, but if you think we're okay. . ."

Jeff frowned at his watch and pushed a button on the side of it. "We're making pretty good time." He eyed Rascal critically. "Your horse seems to be taking it all right. Let him get a drink, and we'll head out. But if you think you need to slow down give a whistle. That goes for you, too," he said to Ruby as she led Lancelot up from the water.

"Well, we are in a race." Ruby moved her palomino back up to the trail. "I don't want Lancelot to be exhausted by the halfway point. He's doing pretty well, actually. He's not even sweating yet."

"You're right about not overdoing it. The horses' condition is what matters. But sometimes our expectations of what a horse can do are too low."

"True," she said. "I don't want to hold you and Chuck back, though. So far we're okay."

When Rascal had finished his drink, Chuck took him back up to the trail. Ruby was mounting, and Jeff had already begun to trot off toward the hills. Chuck hopped into the saddle and smiled at Ruby.

"Ready?"

She nodded. "I was thinking how crazy I was to agree to stay with Jeff. Lancelot and I could be ambling along at our leisure instead of pushing to keep up with the champ. But Lancelot seems to be doing fine."

"If you want to drop back and let Jeff go on ahead. . ." As he spoke, Chuck realized he was beginning to feel like a frontrunner. He didn't want to give up the lead they'd maintained so far.

"You know I'm not in this to win. I just want to finish the course with Lancelot in good condition. But. . ." She looked his Appaloosa over. "How's Rascal doing?"

"He seems to be enjoying himself so far. Hey, wouldn't it be great to finish your first hundred-miler in the top ten?"

She grinned and gathered her reins. "Let's go!"

eight

At the first checkpoint they trotted in together. Chuck was pleased with the way Rascal still pranced and tossed his head at the waiting officials after having gone ten miles. Jeff reined Annabelle in at the last second and gestured for Ruby to precede him across the line.

"Going to keep the one-two-three order?" the ride secretary's assistant asked with a grin as Ruby dismounted.

"Why not?" Jeff hopped down and stood aside, holding Annabelle's reins and watching the back trail.

Ruby held Lancelot's head while the secretary took his pulse. "You're good." She jotted the precise time down on Ruby's vet card. "Just take your horse over there, and the vet will do the exam." On duty was Dr. Philip Nickerson, whom Chuck had met on several occasions.

The secretary checked Rascal's pulse next, then Annabelle's. All were within the acceptable range, and they proceeded to the square where the veterinarian evaluated each horse.

"I only caught one glimpse of a rider behind us," Chuck told Jeff. "That was back on that steep grade where we could see the trail below."

Jeff nodded. "We've got a good lead. Three minutes so far, and no one else in sight. That means we've increased our starting lead."

Chuck inhaled deeply and smiled. It felt great.

"You're good to go when your mandatory fifteen minutes are up, Miss Dale," Dr. Nickerson said, giving Lancelot a slap on the side. "Take this boy over to the start now if you like. Hi, Chuck. How you doing? Having fun?" Nickerson didn't wait for an answer but put his stethoscope to Rascal's ribs just forward of the saddle's cinch strap.

"Oh, yeah," Chuck said with a grin.

"Ruby," Jeff called, and she turned to look at him.

Jeff pointed across the clearing to where a red pickup truck was pulling in. "My crew just arrived."

"You have a crew?" Her eyes widened.

Jeff laughed. "Yeah, my kid brother and a couple of friends. I didn't think they'd make it until the lunch stop, but there they are. Go over and get some water for you and Lancelot. They've got hay and electrolytes for the horses and snacks for us."

"Wow. Thanks, Jeff." Ruby studied Jeff for a long moment before she moved away.

"Trot him out, please," the vet said, and Chuck realized the doctor had already taken Rascal's pulse and counted his respirations. He gripped the lead line and ran beside Rascal for several yards away from the vet then turned him and trotted back.

By the time Dr. Nickerson had finished his examination, given Chuck the go-ahead and teased him gently about his beautiful riding partner, Ruby was walking toward him holding three dripping bottles of water.

"Oh, that looks good." Chuck took one, uncapped it, and tipped his head back for a deep swallow. "Thanks."

"You're welcome. Bring Rascal over. Jeff's friends will sponge him down for you."

"Wow! I don't think he's even hot yet, but that will sure come in handy later on."

Ruby nodded, and her brown eyes glittered. "The secretary

says we've made good time. Not record-breaking time, but pretty good." She glanced toward where the trail entered the mountainside meadow. "Hey, here comes number 4."

Chuck looked over toward the path. "Sure enough."

Jeff eased around Annabelle's head, still holding her reins as Dr. Nickerson counted her respirations. "Eight minutes. We three checked in eight minutes before number 4. Not bad." He winked at Ruby. "You and your golden boy are potential winners."

Ruby flushed. "Oh, I doubt it." She handed Jeff a bottle of water.

"Thanks. As long as you're ahead of the pack, the possibility is there."

Chuck watched Ruby closely. Of course hearing that from a champion was flattering, but Ruby just shrugged. "I'm having a blast."

Jeff laughed. "How about you, Doc? Glad you came?"

"Oh, yeah." Chuck smiled at him. "Don't feel you have to stick with us, though, Jeff. We know you'll want to move out at some point and increase your lead. Don't worry about us. Ruby and I will keep on as fast as we can, but we don't expect to cross the finish line with you."

"You never know. We could finish as the Three Amigos."

Jeff's brilliant smile made even Chuck feel it might be possible. Was Jeff humoring them? Did he do this every year—pick up some trail buddies to pace himself with? Or were Rascal and Lancelot truly among the best competitors today? The other possibility—that Jeff wanted to stick close to Ruby in a bid to win her affections—still niggled at Chuck. Jeff's earlier comment about Chuck having already won should have put that thought to rest, but Chuck couldn't help thinking some of Jeff's laughing remarks to Ruby constituted flirting.

Her wistful expression tugged at his heart. When she turned her gaze from Jeff to him, Chuck's stomach fluttered.

Dr. Nickerson dismissed Annabelle, and Jeff led the mare quickly toward his crew. They tended to the horse while Jeff grabbed a chocolate bar and offered one to Chuck and Ruby.

"Not now," Ruby said. "Maybe later."

"Are you ready to go on?" Chuck asked. "Your hold time is almost up."

"Yeah." She took another swallow of water and looked about.

"I'll take that for you." He'd spotted a trash can near the secretary's booth, set up under an awning beside a small RV. "Mount up, gal."

When he returned from discarding the bottles, Jeff and Ruby were both in the saddle.

"Hurry up, Chuck," Jeff said. "We all checked in at the same time. They're letting us go together, as long as we leave in the order we came in."

"Great!" Chuck swung up onto Rascal's back and eased in between Jeff and Ruby. The fourth rider's horse was in the veterinarian's exam area. "Okay, Ruby, lead us on to victory."

They all waved to Jeff's crew.

"Thanks! We'll see you at Mile 20," Jeff called to his brother. The secretary's assistant stood at the checkpoint's starting line with clipboard and stopwatch in hand.

"Ready. Set. Rider 1, go!"

Ruby grinned at Chuck and urged Lancelot onto the trail at a trot. Chuck moved Rascal forward and the woman with the clipboard said, "Rider 2, go."

Chuck tapped Rascal's sides, and the Appaloosa bunched his muscles and bounded forward.

⁂

The trail angled upward more sharply now, slowing their

pace and causing the horses to breathe faster. Ruby stroked Lancelot's withers and spoke to him frequently, encouraging him to trot when the path wasn't too steep. After a mile she pulled aside in a clearing and let the two men bring their mounts up even with hers. She'd feel better if someone else took the lead.

"One of you go first," she said, looking from Chuck to Jeff and not wanting to make the choice.

"Why don't you take the lead, Jeff?" Chuck smiled at the champ.

"You sure?" Jeff asked.

"It would be a relief," Ruby admitted. "I keep wondering if I should speed up or slow down. You have so much experience that I'd appreciate it if you set the pace for a while."

Chuck didn't seem to mind. His blue eyes held a gleam of satisfaction. "Do you need to rest?" he asked.

Ruby shook her head. "We're good to go, right, fella?" She slapped Lancelot's neck, and he tossed his head as though nodding in agreement.

"Ah, you have a trick horse." Jeff grinned and turned Annabelle forward. "Let's move, amigos!"

His quick start surprised Ruby, but she let Lancelot trot to keep up. A quarter mile later they left the trees behind and embarked on a rougher uphill section. The next two hours required a cautious pace. When they reached the Mile 20 checkpoint, in a ravine below a waterfall, all were ready for a breather. Jeff dismounted when he rode into the hold area and took Annabelle's pulse. Ruby had fallen back a hundred yards, but when Lancelot reached the spot she, too, climbed out of the saddle.

"How you doing?" Jeff asked.

"I'm a little stiff." She did a quick pulse check on her gelding then sat on the dry grass, holding the end of Lancelot's reins and counting his respirations. "That last upgrade was tough. Doesn't the trail dip down next?"

"Right. We'll go all the way down to the valley floor and over the stream. Then there're a couple of miles of fairly flat terrain before we go up another hillside. Guess I'm ready."

Allison Bowie, the ride secretary, was on hand to do the initial gate checks in person.

"All of the riders must have left the starting gate on schedule, or you wouldn't be here now," Ruby said.

"Actually I left Tom in charge at the starting area after the first forty riders took off, and I just pulled in here a minute ago. You guys are fast." Allison smiled at Jeff and wrote the time on his vet card. "You're fine to proceed to the vet check. Your thirty-minute hold starts now."

"Great." Jeff turned to Ruby. "Tell Chuck to go over there where my brother's truck is after he checks in."

Chuck and Rascal walked the last few yards to their resting place while Allison checked Lancelot. Chuck dropped to the ground and removed his hat. "Whew." He wiped his forehead with his sleeve. "Well, we're almost a quarter done. I feel like I've already had quite a workout."

Ruby nodded soberly. "Lancelot's still eager, but I think the rest will do him good. Jeff says to join him and his crew." She pointed to where the young people who'd helped them at Mile 10 were already stripping off Annabelle's tack.

"That's really nice of him. I was counting on amenities at the noon stop but not at every checkpoint."

"I know. It seems kind of strange to me he'd help us so much."

Allison took Ruby's card. "Your horse looks good. And that's just Jeff. He's generous, and he loves the sport. He's always encouraging other riders. This year I guess you're his protégées. Be thankful."

"I don't want to hold him back."

Allison shook her head. "Don't worry about that. Jeff aims for a consistent pace all day long, not a breakneck race. If he thinks you're too slow he'll go on without you. But it's my guess if that happens he'll tell his crew to take care of you if they can do it and still be on time to meet him at the next stop."

Ruby smiled as Allison handed her card back. "He's an all-around nice guy, I guess. Thanks a lot. Chuck, I'll see you in a minute."

She led Lancelot to the veterinarian's station.

"So number 1 has dropped to number 2," the doctor said with a chuckle.

As he began his examination, Ruby looked toward where Jeff had taken Annabelle. The mare was browsing at a flake of hay hung in a net from the truck. Meanwhile three people were sponging her back and legs with cool water. Jeff was nowhere in sight.

When Lancelot's exam was completed she led him slowly toward the truck. As she approached, Jeff came from the direction of the secretary's booth.

"Hey, Ruby! We're doing pretty good. Come on over and meet my gang. Sorry we didn't have time for introductions earlier."

She followed him to the truck. His brother, another young man, and a girl who looked to be about twenty paused in their ministrations to Annabelle.

"Hey, y'all, this is Ruby," Jeff said. "Ruby, this is my brother, Kevin, and his friends, Billy and Kaye."

The young men said hi, and the girl named Kaye gave her

a friendly grin. "Glad to meet you, Ruby. Terrific horse."

"Thanks."

"She and Chuck are good friends of mine," Jeff said, "so hop to and help her get Lancelot comfortable."

The three immediately surrounded Lancelot and began removing his tack. Ruby started to protest but decided that would be foolish. Jeff wanted to do this, and it would be a big help.

"His halter and lead rope are in the pack," she said.

"Terrific." Kevin located them and had Lancelot tethered to the back of his truck in seconds, with a flake of hay shaken out on the tailgate. Kaye brushed Lancelot down, and Billy followed with a bucket of water and sponge.

"You guys are great," Ruby said.

"I trained them well," Jeff told her. "Of course, when Kevin performs in his next rodeo I have to be there to patch him up."

"So you guys do for each other? That's neat."

"It's kept us close." Jeff turned and nodded toward the secretary's booth. "Facilities over there, if you need 'em. Then we've got cold drinks and snacks. I'll wait here for Chuck. Looks like he's heading over here now."

Ruby looked up into his eyes. "I really appreciate what you're doing for Chuck and me."

"I like horses, and I like people." Jeff shrugged. "That's one of the best things about these rides—making new friends."

In the next fifteen minutes Ruby made a point of chatting with Kaye and the two boys and thanking them for the extra effort they put in on Lancelot and Rascal.

"No problem," Kaye assured her. "This is a lark, compared to watching Kevin get tossed off a bull." She wasn't beautiful, but with her short auburn hair, pleasant features and long legs Ruby could see why Kevin liked her so much. His deference to Kaye left no doubt she was Kevin's girl, and Billy was just along for the ride.

"How long have you been seeing Kevin?" Ruby asked.

"Almost a year. He's talking about making it permanent, but I haven't decided yet whether I want to be a young widow or not."

Ruby grimaced. "That bad?"

"When he's good he's very good." Kaye shrugged. "But no cowboy has a good ride every time."

"Well, maybe you'll end up spending your retirement with a crippled old bull rider."

"Yeah, that could happen. Might not be so bad. Now if Jeff could talk him into retiring from rodeo and staying home to help run the ranch I'd like that." Kaye checked her watch and called, "Hey, fellas, time to tack up. Jeff's hold expires in five minutes."

"Let's move," Jeff agreed. "Don't try to go to the next checkpoint. The road's too rough to drive up in there."

"Right," Kevin said. "We'll go refill the water jugs and wait for you at the hold after that."

"Yeah, they'll only have a timekeeper and a vet at Mile 30. You have the map, right?" Jeff asked. "The lunch stop is right where they had it last year."

"Oh, right." Kevin nodded. "Got it. We'll see you there."

"Some of my family will be there," Ruby said. "Look for my folks and two grandmas in a Jeep."

"Jeff, better mount," Billy called. He and Kaye had completed their preparations on Annabelle, and he handed Jeff the reins.

"Thanks," Jeff said. "Now make sure Ruby and Chuck take off right behind me."

The three young people scurried about with brushes,

blankets, and saddles. Two minutes later Ruby mounted and waved to the trio of helpers.

"You guys are the greatest. Thanks!"

Chuck nodded and grinned at her as she turned Lancelot toward the starting area.

The ten miles to the next checkpoint tested all three horses' stamina. At one point Jeff dismounted and walked behind Annabelle as she walked up a steep, rocky grade. At the top of the slope he remounted and waved down at Ruby.

"Take your time. Let him set his own pace."

She nodded and dismounted. "Okay, boy. Up you go." She draped the palomino's reins over his neck and released him. Lancelot eyed her for a moment. "Go on." She thumped his flank, and he stepped out on the upslope.

High above them Annabelle whinnied, and Lancelot pricked up his ears. Had Jeff taught his horse to neigh on command? It certainly put a spring in Lancelot's step. Ruby rushed after him, grabbing rocks and brush for handholds. She caught up to her horse and seized a handful of his tail hair, letting him pull her along without taking too much of her weight. Holding on to his tail helped her stay upright as they climbed. She wondered how Chuck was doing but determined not to look back until they'd made it safely to the top. She couldn't see past Lancelot's hindquarters to tell whether Jeff and Annabelle still watched her ascent.

At last they reached the summit, and her horse pushed onto the flatter area, taking Ruby with him.

"Good job!" Jeff reached out his hand and pulled her farther from the edge of the steep path.

"Thanks." Ruby seized Lancelot's reins and allowed him to edge over closer to Annabelle.

"Look down there." Jeff nodded at the back trail, and Ruby

followed where he pointed.

Chuck and Rascal were only a few yards below them on the trail, with Chuck leading his Appaloosa.

"Wow, they're moving right along," Ruby said. "You don't have to wait for us, Jeff."

"That's okay. But you'd better move Lancelot a little farther away so Chuck has room to maneuver here."

Chuck and his horse scrambled to the top, and Jeff reached for Rascal's bridle.

"Super. You okay?"

"Yeah." Chuck took off his hat, wiped his brow and put it back on. "Whew. Let's hope that was the worst stretch."

Jeff's boyish smile made Ruby want to laugh. "Now comes the fun part. Down to the valley again. But on the way we stop at Mile 30. It's just a little farther now."

"A fifteen-minute breather," Ruby said.

"Right. Let's go." Chuck raised his foot to his stirrup.

"Do you need a boost?" Jeff asked Ruby.

"No, I'm good." She hopped up into the saddle and gathered the reins.

"Well, you're so chipper, maybe you want to lead again." Jeff smiled and arched his eyebrows as he scooped up Annabelle's reins.

Ruby nearly refused, but Chuck grinned and gave her a thumbs-up. She turned Lancelot toward the next checkpoint.

"One-two-three, still leading," the secretary at the cramped Mile 30 holding area said when they rode in. Ruby missed having Kevin and his friends handy with cold drinks, but she actually rested more than she had at the last stop. After their vet checks she sat quietly with Chuck and Jeff for a few minutes, holding the end of Lancelot's lead rope and letting him breathe and snatch wisps of dry grass.

"There's number 5," Chuck observed, nodding to the clearing's entry.

"He passed number 4." Jeff checked his watch. "And he's only three minutes behind us. He must have flown up that steep grade."

Their horses all passed the exam and were ready to start at the earliest opportunity. Ruby was glad. She didn't like number 5, a young man on a chestnut mare, gaining on them so suddenly.

The next few miles of trail were easier as they regained the valley floor. They trotted forward until they came to an open stretch of plains. All the horses broke into a canter, running abreast across the prairie until they picked up the path where it again entered the woods and ducked beneath a railroad bridge.

Ruby looked back but couldn't see any other riders. "How are we doing?" she called to Jeff.

"Middlin'. Are you up for another canter?"

"Rascal's okay," Chuck said.

Ruby nodded. "Let's do it."

Following the trail up a gradual slope, they wound around a gentle hillside. They reached the Mile 40 checkpoint still in the lead. Ruby was startled to see a police car in the field near where the secretary's booth and RV were set up. She spotted her parents, waving wildly to her as she led Lancelot to the veterinarian's station. Kevin Tavish and his friends were parked beside her dad, ready to help during the hour-long noon stop. Kaye was filling a hay net, and Billy carried two buckets of water toward the back of the rig.

Dr. John Hogan met them at the veterinary check with a jovial smile.

"Well, well. Still in the running."

"Hello, Dr. Hogan. Great to see you," Ruby said. The September sun shone brightly on the field, and she felt warm, though they were at least a thousand feet above sea level.

Chuck brought Rascal over to wait while his partner examined Lancelot. "We survived the first forty miles, John."

"That's a relief to me," Hogan shot back. "I'd hate to have to break in a new partner."

As soon as Lancelot was released from his exam, Ruby led him toward Kevin's pickup. She placed the reins in Kaye's hands.

"Thank you so much!"

"Relax and have something to eat," Kaye said. "We'll take good care of this guy."

"Great. My folks are right over there, so Chuck and I are going to eat lunch with them." She turned toward the Jeep. Her parents, with Grandma, Elsie Daniels and her cousin Dylan, waved and grinned.

"Come on, Ruby," her father called.

As she walked toward them smiling, the police officer and another man approached her.

"Miss Dale?"

"Yes."

The officer nodded toward the man who accompanied him. "This is George Ware. He's the fire marshal, and he'd like to ask you a few questions."

nine

As Chuck held Rascal still for the veterinary exam, he watched Ruby lead her palomino away. This would be a highpoint of the day for her, he could tell. Her eyes had gleamed when she spied her parents waiting for her.

A police officer and another man intercepted her after she'd turned Lancelot over to Jeff's crew. More about the fire?

"Trot him out," Dr. Hogan said.

Chuck obeyed, keeping his eye on Ruby. When John released him with a favorable report, he hurried across the field. Now Ruby was over near her Jeep, hugging her parents. But the two men waited a few yards away, so it wasn't over yet.

"Hey, Chuck!" Billy jogged out to meet him. "Want me to take Rascal for you? Ruby said you're eating lunch with her and her family."

"Sure. Thanks a lot."

"We'll take good care of him. You can count on that."

Chuck smiled in acknowledgment and let him take the reins. When he turned toward the Dales' parking spot, Ruby was hugging a white-haired woman. That must be Grandma. He heard Ruby say, "Did you all hear about the fire at the starting booth this morning?"

"No," said her dad. "What happened?"

"I'll have to tell you later." She looked up and spotted him. "Oh, here comes Chuck. He can tell you. I need to go speak to the fire marshal." Their bewildered glances landed on Chuck. Ruby winced and said to him, "Do you mind explaining to Mom and Dad why I have to go talk to that cop and the fire marshal?"

"Sure."

"Thanks."

She hurried back to the waiting men.

Chuck turned to Martin Dale.

"What happened?" Martin demanded.

"Ruby's all right. There was a fire this morning at the starting area. She was the first to arrive, and she reported it. The fire chief told us it was arson and that the fire marshal would want to talk to her later. I think that's what this is about."

"Was anyone hurt?" Ruby's mother asked.

"No. The registration booth burned, and there was some damage to a shed the riding club had out there to hold supplies. Nothing serious."

"Well, let's get out the lunch so we'll be ready when Ruby's done," the older woman said. "By the way, I'm Ruby's grandma."

"Pleased to meet you." Chuck shook her hand with a grin.

"And this is my sister-in-law, Elsie," Grandma added. "Say, Linda, where did you put the paper plates?"

Ruby's mother turned to help her find the picnic settings.

"Who are those kids wiping Ruby's horse down?" Martin asked.

"Oh, those are some new friends." Chuck grinned and nodded toward Jeff, who was leading Annabelle across the field. "See that guy in the red shirt?"

"How could I miss him?"

Chuck laughed. "Well, that's the two-year champion, Jeff Tavish. Ruby and I have been riding with him. His brother and a couple of friends insist on taking care of our horses along with Jeff's."

"That's mighty nice," Martin said.

"Yeah."

Jeff caught Chuck's eye and waved.

"Say, we've got a ton of food," Linda said. "Maybe we should invite them to join us?" She shook out a quilt and spread it on the dead grass.

When Ruby joined them a few minutes later, Jeff had brought the cooler over from his truck and pooled his party's food with the Dales'.

"Wow! Is this a feast?" Ruby asked.

"Almost." Chuck stood until she'd chosen a corner of the quilt and sat down.

"Did you meet everyone?" she asked as he settled down beside her.

"I think we did." Chuck smiled at her parents, Elsie, Grandma, and Dylan.

"You've got a great family," Jeff said. "Can't believe your lovely grandma Margaret drives a trailer truck."

Grandma grinned at him. "Oh, you're a charmer—I can see that."

Linda looked toward Jeff's rig. "Should we wait for your friends?"

"Naw," Jeff replied. "They said they'll come over after they're finished grooming the three horses. I told them we'd save them each a chicken bone."

Martin let out a guffaw then sobered. "Right. Let's pray then." He closed his eyes and began to ask the blessing.

Chuck quickly bowed his head without looking to see Jeff's reaction. As soon as Martin said, "Amen," food containers came at him rapidly from both sides. He filled his plate with sandwiches, fried chicken, potato chips. and fruit salad. Grandma passed him a can of soda.

"So, Ruby, what did the police want?" her mother asked. "Was it about that fire?"

Ruby nodded. "I had to tell the fire marshal everything I told the fire chief this morning. And the police want me to go to the police station tonight when the ride is over to look at some pictures."

"Pictures?" Her father eyed her closely.

"Yeah, I saw a man in a pickup leaving the field this morning right before I discovered the fire. They hope I can recognize him in a photo lineup."

"That's exciting," said Grandma. "Can I go with you?"

Ruby laughed and leaned over to hug her. "It will probably be late, Gram, but thanks. You always keep me laughing, you know that?"

"Well, at the rate we're moving today," Jeff said, "Ruby will probably make it to the police station by nine o'clock."

"Thanks, Jeff." Ruby's brow puckered as she sipped her soft drink. "I told them I probably won't be able to get there until Sunday. We could be on the trail until well after midnight, depending on how Lancelot holds up."

Chuck noticed her frown remained in spite of the conversation that swirled around them about horses and Kevin's next rodeo performance. He leaned close to her ear and asked, "Do you want to drop out? I could take you to the police station now."

She chuckled. "I'd accuse you of trying to eliminate the competition, but that would take you out of the race, too. No, seriously, they said it's all right. It's just a little creepy, not knowing if the man I saw was the arsonist. I keep thinking of things I could have done differently."

"Don't. You did just fine."

"So are you guys, like, winning this thing?" Dylan asked.

Chuck had learned he was in his senior year of high school and the oldest of Ruby's cousins.

Ruby turned with sparkling brown eyes. "As of right now we sure are."

"Rider number 5 checked in three minutes behind me," Jeff said. "Ruby, you need to be ready when the hour's up."

She consulted her watch. "We've still got twenty-eight minutes. Guess I have time for one of Mom's apple turnovers."

❧

Chuck was surprised how easy the next fifteen miles seemed. Rascal stepped along as jauntily as he had at seven that morning. The trail took them deep into the hills. After a fifteen-minute hold at Mile 51 the three frontrunners sped along toward the log bridge near the junction with the old stagecoach road. Kevin, Billy, and Kaye had promised to meet them at the new Mile 63 checkpoint where the loop added this year rejoined the traditional trail.

Chuck had taken the lead, and Rascal snorted disdainfully as he approached the span over a rushing stream. He plodded steadily over it, and Ruby took Lancelot along behind him with no problems, though his hoofbeats thunked loud and hollow on the planks and the whitewater gushed over the rocks below them. Chuck looked back again in time to see Jeff and Annabelle also crossing with ease.

"This is it," Ruby called to Jeff. "We pick up the old stagecoach road here."

Jeff's eyes glittered as they turned onto the new section of the trail. Chuck felt the exhilaration, too. The path was wider and somewhat easier than the last stretch had been, and he was able to relax in the saddle and take in the vistas from every vantage point. A cool breeze off the summit reminded him winter came early in the mountains. He stopped for a minute to untie his light jacket from the back of Rascal's saddle.

"Getting chilly up here," he said to Ruby as she came abreast of him.

"Yeah, it is." She reached for her hooded sweatshirt, and Jeff pulled a denim jacket from the back of his saddle.

All too soon they reached a downhill section where places in the trail had eroded. The dicey footing required caution as they wound around the mountainside.

"This is one section Ruby and I walked yesterday," Chuck told Jeff. "Too rough to drive up, even with her Jeep."

At one point a rock slide had narrowed the trail so they had to pick their way through slowly, one behind the other.

At last they came down to the junction and the rest stop. Kevin, Billy, and Kaye were there, ready with water buckets, sweat scrapes, and cool drinks. Chuck peeled off his jacket and stowed it again, and Ruby did the same with her sweatshirt.

After turning Rascal over to the crew, Chuck chose a bottle of water. Ruby was still at the vet check, and Jeff had disappeared toward the secretary's booth for news. Chuck walked over near the rim of the trail where he and Ruby had eaten their lunch Friday and seen the riders below. All the action seemed to be up here on the mountain today. He took a long swig of water.

"No horses tied up down there?" Ruby stepped up beside him and peered down into the ravine.

"Nope. Nary a one."

She smiled faintly but continued to search the wooded area below.

"I looked over my maps last night," Chuck said. "I couldn't find any trails or old roads down in that area."

Ruby shook her head slightly. "I don't know why I keep

thinking about it. Hey, it must be almost time for you to saddle up."

Two riders entered the rest stop before Chuck mounted, with number 5 being closest behind them. The young man on the chestnut mare was now six minutes behind them, and number 8, Tom and Hester Marden's daughter, Reagan, came in two minutes after him.

"How's it going back there?" Jeff called to Reagan as she held her horse for the initial check-in.

"Not bad," the young woman replied. "I think they've bunched up a little. Hey, that stagecoach road was a fantastic ride!"

They were still talking when the secretary's assistant gave Chuck the nod.

"Rider number 2, go."

He looked over at Ruby, who was next in line on Lancelot, gave her a wave, and headed out. Immediately the timekeeper called, "Rider number 1, go."

Chuck let Rascal trot out confidently, but after the first mile he pulled over to the side at a wide spot in the trail.

Ruby brought her horse up beside his. "This is where we agreed Jeff should take the lead?"

Chuck nodded. "He said it's one of the most treacherous parts of the trail. I'd as soon have the champ go first."

Ruby looked back at Jeff and Annabelle, who trotted toward them. "He's done it several times. I'd rather follow him, too."

"All set?" Jeff called as he came even with them.

"Yeah," said Chuck. "Go ahead, and we'll be right behind you."

He urged Ruby to precede him and fell in last. The trail soon narrowed between a sheer cliff towering above them on their left and a sparse stand of spruce on their right. Through the trees he could see a distant line of mountains. The horses walked, conserving energy on the slight uphill grade.

They left the trees behind, and suddenly the rim of the mountainside dropped away on their right. At least there was plenty of room to continue safely in single file. Bright orange flags along the edge of the trail warned the riders to keep their distance.

Ruby turned around in her saddle and called, "We must be right above that rock slide where the hikers went yesterday."

Chuck squinted and looked out over the valley. "Maybe. I think we're past that now."

They rounded a bend, and ahead of them Jeff had paused to give Annabelle a breather and observe the view. His bay mare stood with her front feet closer to the edge than Chuck would have liked. Ruby halted her horse a few yards back, and Rascal stopped of his own accord behind Lancelot.

"Are we holding you back?" Ruby called to Jeff.

"Nah, Annabelle needed a little rest. We're pulling some serious altitude here."

Ruby nodded. She looked over at Chuck and smiled. "I almost think I want my sweatshirt again. It's cool up here." She swiveled in the saddle and tugged at her cantle pack.

"Let me get that." Chuck prodded Rascal to slide over closer to the palomino and opened Ruby's pack with it still tied in place. He pulled out her navy-blue zippered sweatshirt. "Here you go."

"Thanks." She took it and slipped her arms into the sleeves while he fastened the buckle on her pack.

He was about to comment on the drop in temperature when a quick scuffling movement drew his attention to Jeff and Annabelle. As he looked up, Chuck's heart leaped into his throat. A large hawk swooped just over Jeff's head, flapping its wings near the horse's ears. Annabelle leaped back and shied to the side, flinging Jeff over her left side. He hung on to the saddle but fought a losing battle with gravity. The horse's near hind foot slipped over the edge of the rocky path, and she stumbled, taking Jeff down nearly to the ground. Annabelle snorted and strained to regain her footing, but her struggle only caused her other hind hoof to loosen small rocks as she clawed to get purchase, one foot still dangling over the rim.

"Jeff!" Ruby cried. The hawk glided off over the valley, oblivious to Jeff's plight.

Chuck shoved his reins toward Ruby and bailed out of his saddle. He ran toward Annabelle, hoping to seize her reins and steady the mare.

Jeff's face melted from consternation to fear as he slid lower along the mare's side and gave up the fight to stay in the flat saddle. He pushed off and dove down the near side, landing with a thud on the edge of the rocky trail, just inches from the precipice. His hat flew off and landed a yard away. Before he could roll out of Annabelle's way and away from the edge, the mare heaved herself forward in a desperate lunge. Free of Jeff's cumbersome weight, she leaped up, scrabbling with her hind feet.

Just as Chuck reached her head, Annabelle found a foothold with her back hoof and jumped onto solid ground, landing low on her hocks, with her haunches sticking out behind. The whites showed around the mare's eyes, and she gasped for breath, emitting a shrill squeal. In a last bid for safety she swung sideways, her hind feet swinging around and knocking Jeff toward the edge.

Chuck seized the reins and pulled her forward, hearing

Ruby's scream as he hauled Annabelle toward the high cliff face on the other side of the trail. He whirled her around, stroking her neck.

"Easy, girl." He looked back toward the edge of the trail.

Jeff was gone.

ten

"What happened?" Chuck stared at the edge of the trail where Jeff had lain a moment before.

Ruby's stomach heaved, and her head seemed to spin. "He. . . he went over. When Annabelle jumped up, she kicked him."

Chuck's face crumpled for a moment; then he straightened his shoulders.

Rascal snorted and crowded against Lancelot. The palomino responded by nipping at Rascal's face.

"Can you come get Annabelle?" Chuck called. "Hurry."

Ruby pulled Lancelot's head around, away from Rascal's. She looped Rascal's reins over her right hand and squeezed her palomino's sides. "Come on, boy. Move."

"Hold on. I've got something here." Chuck looped Annabelle's reins around a projection of rock. "Be good, girl."

Ruby dismounted and dropped Lancelot's reins. He would stay put, and he was in a broad spot on the trail where he would be safe. She wasn't sure Rascal would ground tie, so she led him forward. Chuck was already at the edge of the trail, lying prone and looking over the rim.

"Can you see him?" Ruby asked.

After an agonizing moment Chuck said, "Yeah. He's about forty feet down, and he's crunched up against a scrub pine." He put his hands up to his face to form a megaphone. "Hey, Jeff! Can you hear me?"

Ruby held her breath.

"Yeah!" Chuck let out a short laugh and waved. "Hey, buddy,

don't try to move. We'll get you some help."

. "Is he all right?" Ruby didn't see how that was possible.

Chuck shredded her temporary relief when he pushed back away from the edge and stood. "No. I think he's hurt bad, but he moved his arm. I've got to get down there."

"It's really steep."

He nodded. "It's not sheer, but it's too steep to maneuver without help. I don't want to end up hurt as badly as Jeff is. He probably fell the first five yards then slid the rest of the way. Do we have any rope?"

"I have Lancelot's lead line."

"And I've got Rascal's. Jeff has one, too, I think. I'll check his pack. If we tie them all together, I may be able to use them to lower myself down past the worst of it, to where it's not quite so bad."

Ruby picked up Jeff's hat and hurried back to Lancelot, tugging impatiently at Rascal's bridle so that he followed her. While she opened her pack to get her lead line Rascal nipped her palomino's flank, and Lancelot squealed and kicked at him.

"Would you two stop it! You're supposed to be friends." Ruby slapped Rascal's nose and put his reins in her other hand, struggling to fish the eight-foot nylon lead line from her cantle pack.

"You have your phone, right?" Chuck called.

"Yeah." She looked over at him. He'd found a cotton rope in Jeff's saddle pack. "I don't know if I can get a connection up here."

"Try." Chuck walked toward her and reached for Rascal's saddle. "I'll tie all the lines together, but I doubt they'll reach more than twenty feet once I put knots in them."

Ruby's hands shook as she handed him Lancelot's lead.

Chuck tied the end of her line to his own and pulled at the knot to test it.

"Guess I'll tie a loop in Jeff's and clip the snap to it."

Ruby dug in the pack for her cell phone. When she found it she pushed the button to turn it on. While she waited for the screen to clear she hugged herself, trying to stop her shivering. "What if the snap breaks?"

He shrugged. "It's supposedly strong enough to hold a horse. I'll have to take the risk. It would take too long to get someone to hike in from the mouth of the canyon and climb up to him. We're not even sure where the nearest road is."

"There might be an easier path somewhere along here."

"Yeah. But time may be critical, Ruby." He walked to the edge of the trail again and lay down with his head sticking out over the drop. After a long moment he stood.

"He's lying right where he was when I first saw him. I need to get down there."

Ruby studied the screen on her phone and frowned. "No bars. I don't think I can reach anyone, Chuck."

He frowned and glanced up the trail. "Maybe if you go up a little farther."

"Or maybe I should take Lancelot and ride back to the checkpoint."

"Well. . .it's closer than the next one." Chuck gritted his teeth.

Ruby knew she couldn't ride off for help and leave Chuck to climb down there alone with no one spotting for him.

Lord, help us!

"Are you praying?" she asked him.

"Yeah. Big-time. Run up to the top of the rise and try your phone from there."

Ruby dashed up the path, praying silently as she ran. At

the highest point she stopped and looked at her phone.

"Maybe. Please, God." She pushed 911 and listened, trying to still her ragged breathing.

"What is your emergency?"

Ruby's knees almost buckled at the sound of the familiar voice.

"Nadine! It's Ruby. I'm at the hundred-mile ride, and we've had an accident."

"What's up?"

"One of the riders fell off a cliff. We're trying to get down to him, but we need rescue fast."

"What's the 20?"

"Between mile markers 65 and 66 on the trail. Drive in at Bear Creek Road. You can get an ambulance within a mile and a half of him. The EMTs will have to walk in from there."

"You're breaking up," Nadine said, "but I think you said Bear Creek Road. Is that correct?"

"Affirmative. There are race officials at the checkpoint. Tell them we're past Mile 65. And we have a veterinarian here who's trying to get down to the victim and give first aid."

"Got it."

Ruby closed her phone and raced back to where she had left Chuck. He looked up from his effort to connect the mismatched lines solidly.

"Did you get through?"

"Yes. They'll send an ambulance to the rest stop."

"Great. Help me find a solid place to tie the end of this. It has to be close to the edge, or there won't be enough length to do me any good."

"Can we tie it to Rascal's saddle horn?"

"Not long enough."

Ruby's stomach roiled. Was Jeff dying while they debated the best way to reach him? "Chuck, I'm lighter than you are."

"So?"

"So I should be the one to climb down the rope."

His eyes narrowed. "No way."

"Yes. Think about it. You could hold the end of the rope. We'd get the maximum length out of it that way."

"Oh, no. I'd probably drop you, or we'd both end up falling down there. Look, Ruby. I have medical training. I know I'm an animal doctor, but. . ."

He looked deep into her eyes, and at last Ruby inhaled and nodded. "You're right."

His smile was only a shadow of the one he'd charmed her with earlier. "Good. We agree. Now when I get down there I want you to take these three horses farther up the trail and hitch them in a safe place. You'll have to tie them by their reins, which isn't good, but it's all we have."

"Okay, but we need signals. When you get down there, you need to let me know how bad it is and if we need a helicopter or what."

"I should be able to make you hear me," Chuck said.

Hoofbeats clattered on the rocky trail behind them, and they both turned toward the sound.

Rider number 5, the young man on the chestnut, trotted into view. He pulled his mare up short when he saw them.

"What's going on?"

"We've got a man down," Chuck replied. "We'll need help."

His eyes widened. "No kidding? Where is he?"

Ruby pointed toward the edge of the trail. "Down there."

The young man's jaw dropped.

"Can you ride back to the checkpoint for help?" Chuck asked.

He hesitated.

"Well, at least help me get down there so I can check him over and give him first aid."

"Sure." He climbed from the saddle and eyed Ruby. "I'm Cody. You're Ruby, right?"

"Yeah." The bib with the bold number 1 felt like a scarlet letter, announcing her identity to the world.

Chuck once more went prone, leaning over the edge of the dropoff. "Cody, there's a stunted tree growing a few yards down the slope over there." He pointed to the left below them. "If you can help Ruby hold the line while I climb down there, I can tie the end to that tree and use the line to get down close to where Jeff is."

Cody's eyes popped open wider than ever. "Jeff Tavish? The champ is down there?"

"That's right."

"Oh, man."

Together they braced themselves. Ruby held the knot where Chuck had hooked the two nylon lines, and Cody grabbed the flat woven strap just below her hands. Chuck tested his weight against it then eased himself gingerly over the edge of the rock.

"Easy. Let it out a little. A little more. I'm almost to the tree."

Ruby gritted her teeth. Her hands hurt, and her arms ached. If not for Cody's help, she was sure she would have flown down the mountainside.

Suddenly the weight lifted.

"I'm at the tree!" Chuck yelled. "Hold on a sec." A moment later he called, "Okay. Let go."

She let the line slide away and clasped her aching hands. Cody went to his knees and peered downward, and Ruby lay on her stomach beside him. Chuck was trying his weight against the line once more. The scrubby tree he'd tied it to looked insubstantial, but it held as he began slowly backing down the steep incline. He reached a place where the hillside spread out more, supporting small brush, and paused to rest against a jagged rock.

He was at the end of the rope. Ruby judged the distance between him and Jeff's crumpled form to be about ten yards. She and Cody watched in silence as Chuck released himself from the line and edged onward, down and over toward Jeff.

Hoofbeats sounded behind them, and Cody leaped up. Reagan Marden trotted around the bend on her pinto gelding.

"Hey! Take it easy! There's been an accident," Cody shouted.

Reagan pulled her horse to a stop near Rascal. "What's up?"

"Jeff Tavish fell over the edge," Ruby said. "Dr. Sullivan is going down to help him, and I called for an ambulance."

"Wow. Anything I can do?"

Ruby looked at the cluster of horses in the trail. "The thing that would help most would be to take our horses a little ways up the trail to where you can tie them up off to one side. The trail is so narrow here that we don't want to clog the path. Someone else could get hurt."

"Sure. Is Jeff hurt bad?"

"We don't know yet. He was moving a little."

The girl nodded. "Oh, I have some aspirin in my saddlebag if it will help."

"I'll take it," Ruby said.

Reagan fished out a small plastic bottle and handed it to her.

"If you can just secure the horses, then you may as well ride on," Ruby told her. "When you get to the next checkpoint, tell them what's happened. I expect the ambulance will arrive at the Bear Creek stop before that, though."

"I could help her," Cody said.

Ruby gritted her teeth and nodded. He didn't want to give up his advantage and let Reagan take the lead in the race. Oh, well. It was a sport, after all.

"Sure. You two go ahead. I'll stay here."

Cody ran to his horse. Ruby watched as he untied Annabelle and led her off up the trail. Reagan hooked Lancelot's reins over Rascal's saddle horn and clucked, pulling Rascal along by his bridle. To Ruby's relief both horses followed her pinto without nipping or kicking.

As the cavalcade disappeared up the trail, she sighed. They were past the most dangerous point now. There was plenty of room, really. If only that hawk hadn't swooped down from the cliff above and startled Annabelle.

She went back to the edge and lay down once more, pulling herself over until she could see down to where Jeff lay. Chuck was beside him now, bending low over Jeff's form. She wanted to yell and ask him for information, but she waited silently, praying for Jeff.

After what seemed like hours, Chuck turned toward her and rose, clinging to the small tree that had broken Jeff's slide down the mountainside.

"Ruby!"

She waved. "Yeah! I hear you."

Chuck nodded.

"How bad is it?" she called.

"Pretty bad. Broken arm for sure, maybe an ankle too, and no doubt heavy internal injuries."

Ruby's heart sank. The pitiful bottle of aspirin Reagan had passed her would do no good and might make things worse if Jeff was bleeding, since aspirin was a blood thinner. "What can I do?"

"Just get the medics down here as quick as you can." He

pointed to her right, along the back trail. "The slope is easier over there. They might be able to come down with a stretcher. I don't see any place a chopper could land, though."

"Okay. I'll see if I can call dispatch and tell them that."

Chuck waved and turned back.

Hoofbeats thudded again on the rocky trail, and Ruby scrambled to her feet and away from the edge.

eleven

Several riders wearing racing bibs trotted toward her. She recognized the woman edging up behind them on a quick-stepping black. Dr. Heather Spelling of Laramie, the veterinarian from the last checkpoint.

"What happened?" asked the first rider who reached her.

"An accident, but help is on the way. The best thing you can do is keep moving." Ruby waved on riders 4, 6, and 9. When they'd continued up the trail the veterinarian rode up to her and dismounted.

"I'm Dr. Spelling. As soon as we got the message, I packed all the supplies I could in a backpack. Where's the patient?"

"Down there." Ruby pointed toward the rim. "Dr. Sullivan is with him. I think you know Chuck?"

"Yes, and I know Jeff Tavish, too. Is there a way for me to get down to them?"

Ruby gritted her teeth. "It's really steep the way Chuck went. We improvised a line for him to hang on to. But he thinks it would be easier if we tried back there a little ways." She pointed. "The slope is more gradual, and you can get down to their level and work your way across."

Dr. Spelling nodded. "I'm not so good with heights, but I'll do it. Can you tie my horse up somewhere? He belongs to one of the ride officials, and I don't want anything to happen to him."

"Sure. But. . ." Ruby looked toward the precipice. "Maybe we could throw your pack down to Chuck, and he could get it and have the supplies while you're working your way down there."

"Good idea. I'll take out anything breakable."

"Let me tell Chuck what you're going to do, and then I'll take your horse." Ruby crept to the edge and lay down again. "Chuck!"

He looked up at her and waved.

"Dr. Spelling is here. Can I throw down a backpack with some bandages and stuff?"

"Terrific. I can use it."

Dr. Spelling crept to her side. "Here. I took out all the glass vials and syringes."

"We can put them in my pack for you to carry," Ruby said.

"Sounds good. Do you want to toss this down there, or shall I?"

"Are you good at softball?" Ruby asked.

Dr. Spelling chuckled. "Lousy at it. You go." She handed over the red backpack. It was light and floppy. Ruby wondered if she could get it near Chuck.

"Hey!" Chuck yelled.

She looked down at him.

"Just toss it gently and let it tumble down."

"What if it doesn't get close enough to you?"

"Then I'll climb up and get it."

Ruby gulped. "Okay." She sent up a swift prayer and threw the pack out away from the edge as far as she could. It plopped to the earth and rolled several yards then came to rest against a projecting rock about eight feet above Chuck and Jeff.

"Perfect," he shouted.

Ruby grimaced. It was far from perfect, but he would act as though it were. She watched as he crawled up the hillside and stretched to retrieve the pack. Pebbles dislodged by his feet pattered down the incline. Dr. Spelling caught her breath, and Ruby waited for something worse to happen. Chuck remained still for a half minute then inched his way back down to Jeff. When he was back at the patient's side Ruby exhaled, backed away from the edge, and stood. Dr. Spelling rose and brushed off her jeans.

"Listen. I could go down," Ruby said. "Let me go tie up your horse with ours and bring back my pack. I'll carry the medications down to Chuck."

"Well. . ."

"I'm sure I can do it."

Dr. Spelling sighed. "I don't have much that will help him. Saline and some painkillers. Most everything I had along was dosed for horses, though. We don't want a medication accident, so I only put in a few drugs."

Ruby reached out to squeeze her arm. "It's okay. I'm glad you rode up here. Just having the bandages will help Chuck a lot. If you stay here and make sure the riders keep going and don't block the trail and show the ambulance personnel where to climb down, it'll be terrific."

The vet still looked skeptical.

"You think about it," Ruby said. "I'll be right back." She jogged up the trail with the coal black horse trotting beside her. Around the next bend Lancelot, Rascal, and Annabelle were tethered off to one side and browsing the meager foliage. She hitched the black near them and ran to Lancelot. "Maybe I should have brought the lead ropes," she muttered, but there was no way she could have gotten them from the scrub pine where Chuck had tied them without climbing down there. With no harness that would be far too dangerous.

She unfastened her cantle pack, checked to make sure

each horse was securely tied, and ran back down the path. Dr. Spelling was talking to rider 11, who sat astride a rangy chestnut. He moved on and passed Ruby.

"Who's doing the vet check now that you're gone?" Ruby asked as she handed her pack to the vet.

"I don't know. Tom Marden said he'd have the vet come up from the third checkpoint as soon as possible. Meanwhile, the secretary's assistant at Mile 63 said she'd check the vital signs and make sure all the horses took their mandatory rest."

"I guess that's all they can do until another vet gets there," Ruby said.

Dr. Spelling pulled vials and syringes from her pockets. "Okay, that's it. Are you sure you want to do this?"

"Yeah, I'm sure."

Ruby took the pack and slung it over her shoulder. She walked back along the trail and scrutinized the terrain below her.

"Hey!"

She looked up when Dr. Spelling called to her. "Yeah?"

"Chuck's pointing farther along. Go farther down the trail."

Ruby nodded and walked several yards back, around a slight curve in the trail. The mountainside was definitely gentler here. She adjusted the pack and prepared to climb down off the path. Another horse came walking up the trail toward her.

"Hey!" called rider 12. "Number 1!"

"Yeah?" Ruby waited for him to come closer.

"I'm supposed to tell you the ambulance was on the way when I left the last checkpoint. The EMTs will be here shortly."

"Great."

"So I heard Jeff Tavish fell off a cliff. Is he alive?"

"Yes." Ruby blinked at him, wondering how much to say and at the same time wishing she had more information to give. "Uh, he's hurt, but we've got two doctors helping him." No need mentioning they were animal doctors.

The rider nodded. "Okay. Guess I'll move along."

"Best thing you can do," Ruby said.

She watched him round the curve and inhaled deeply then stepped down off the trail. Her momentum pulled her downward, and she grabbed at low-growing shrubs to slow her descent.

❧

Chuck knelt beside Jeff, bracing himself on the steep hillside as he rummaged through the backpack Ruby had flung down to him. He pulled out two rolls of gauze and a tube of antibiotic ointment.

"I don't want to move you much, but I need to roll you away from that tree just a little so I can get at your arm."

"Do it."

Chuck pressed gently on Jeff's right wrist to keep the arm from flopping when he moved him and pushed him over, uphill, onto his back. Jeff let out a quick groan then was silent.

"There we go," Chuck said.

Jeff's eyes flickered open. "How we doing?" The champ's words slurred, and he grimaced as he tried to shift his weight.

"Could be worse." Chuck glanced up the hill. No help yet. The arm really needed a splint. "I think we should wrap your ankle while we wait. It's swelling a lot."

"Is it broken?"

"I'm not sure. Could be just a bad sprain. I also think that arm will need to be splinted before you're moved."

"Hurts something wicked."

"I'll bet."

"Annabelle kicked me. Can't believe she spooked like that. Guess I jumped the wrong way when she did." Jeff looked up at the blue sky. "I'm causing a lot of trouble, aren't I? Are we going to need a Life Flight?"

"I'm not sure they could land here," Chuck said. "They could maybe lower a basket stretcher. But I think we can carry you up to the trail."

Jeff turned his head slightly, wincing as he moved. "Up there? I doubt it."

"It's not so bad over yonder." Chuck nodded toward where he'd told Ruby to send the EMTs. "Let's get your ankle wrapped." He'd already removed Jeff's boot, and he began to wind the gauze firmly around the injured ankle.

"Kevin will never let me hear the end of this," Jeff murmured.

Chuck smiled as he worked. "Well, you usually take care of him when he gets banged up in the rodeo, right?"

"Yeah."

"So let him mollycoddle you for a change."

Jeff looked up again toward where he had fallen. "Guess I could have broken my neck, easy as not."

"That's right," Chuck said. "God was watching over you for sure."

Jeff gave a little shrug and grimaced. "Uh! This arm is killing me." He brought his left arm over and grasped his right arm just below the elbow.

"That's broken, no doubt. I'd like to get your jacket off, but I don't want to hurt you, so I figured to leave it for the EMTs to cut off."

Jeff sighed. "My favorite jacket."

"Well, it looks like your arm is bleeding a little." Chuck

frowned at the dark stain on Jeff's sleeve. "Compound fracture, I'm guessing, but I could make it worse if I pull that sleeve off. It's not bleeding hard, I don't think, but it seems to be oozing a little."

"How long have I been here?"

"Fifteen minutes, maybe."

"How long before the EMTs get here?"

"I don't know. Ruby got through to the call center on her cell phone, which is a blessing. I'm guessing it would take them twenty minutes to drive to the last checkpoint and another twenty to hike up here with their equipment."

Jeff bit his upper lip. "Do whatever you think is best, Chuck."

"Well, you're not going to bleed to death. I'm praying they get here soon."

"You and Ruby pray a lot, don't you?"

Chuck eyed him cautiously. "You could say that."

"I guess this wouldn't be a bad time for you to pray for me, if you don't mind."

≈

Ruby had just started along the sloping hillside when her cell phone rang. Rather than try to balance while she talked, she sat down and opened the phone.

"Ruby, this is Nadine. How are you doing?"

"Okay. Is the ambulance on the way?" Ruby could barely believe she was receiving a signal.

"Yes. They're on Bear Creek Road now and should reach the checkpoint you told me about any minute."

"They'll still have a hike ahead of them unless they can borrow horses."

Nadine chuckled. "That would be something. How's the patient?"

"I don't know. I'm heading down there now. Dr. Sullivan is with him, and we threw down some dressings one of the other vets had along."

"Okay. I don't want to run your cell phone down, so I'll let you go, but I wanted to let you know it won't be long before help gets there."

"Thanks." Ruby put her phone away and edged along the rough ground, finding hand and toeholds before letting go of the sagebrush and shrubs that gave her meager support. "Hello," she called as she approached the two men. "I brought you some things Dr. Spelling had in her kit and a canteen and some aspirin if you think it will do Jeff any good. The ambulance should be at the checkpoint by now."

"I'd probably better not medicate him then." Chuck looked up at the trail above, and Dr. Spelling waved at them. "Can you use a drink of water, Jeff?" he asked the patient.

"Yeah, thanks."

Chuck helped lift Jeff's shoulders, and Ruby opened the canteen for him. Jeff took a long drink and moaned as Chuck eased him back to the ground.

"Your arm's bothering you a lot, isn't it?" Chuck asked.

"Yeah."

"He's shivering." Ruby eyed Jeff critically. "I should have brought a blanket down."

"I'm okay." Jeff's chattering teeth belied his statement.

"Here." Chuck pulled off his denim jacket and laid it over Jeff's torso. "I'm wondering if we should immobilize your arm now. It would make things quicker when the EMTs get here."

"How would you do that?" Ruby asked, looking around at the slight vegetation.

"I think I could find a couple of sticks." Chuck pointed

in the opposite direction from where Ruby had come down. "There are a few small trees over there. Say. . ." He stared up the cliff face.

"What are you thinking?" Ruby asked. Jeff lay with his eyes closed, and she wondered if he was asleep or unconscious.

"It's going to be tough getting a stretcher down here and even harder getting it back up. I was thinking that if we could rig a stretcher now and collect enough rope we could use the horses to pull Jeff up to the trail."

Ruby frowned. "That would cut the time to get him to the hospital all right."

"Go for it," Jeff said, his eyes still closed.

Ruby smiled. "So you *are* still awake. I'm just afraid we'd hurt you worse if we bungled the job."

"I think we can do it," Chuck said.

"At least you'll have something to think about while we wait," Jeff said. He opened his eyes and squinted up at Ruby. "You ought to go on to the finish line."

"What? Leave you guys here? No way."

He started to smile but grimaced and drew in a quick breath. "No sense you both losing out on a good chance for the top ten. How many riders have passed us already?"

"Don't know, don't care," Ruby said.

Chuck stood up, balancing carefully on the slope. "If you'll be okay for a few minutes, I'm going to look for some sticks for splints and see if there are any poles long enough to make a stretcher."

Ruby watched him gingerly negotiate the slope until he worked his way down to easier going. They weren't that far beyond where they'd seen the mysterious riders tie their horses the day before.

She smiled down at Jeff. "Hey, champ, if you had to take a

fall I'm glad you didn't do it back where that rock slide was. You'd have broken all two hundred bones in your body."

"Right." A brief smile flickered on Jeff's lips. "I sure didn't mean to cost you and Chuck the ride."

"Don't think about it. We're glad we were there when it happened. It might have been a while before anyone found you."

"Yeah." He was quiet for a moment. "I guess Kevin's going to be worried when we don't show up at the next stop."

"The first riders through will tell him what happened," Ruby said.

Jeff clenched his teeth. "That number 5 will win."

"It's okay." Ruby brushed a strand of damp hair back from his forehead, noting that his brow was wet, even though he shivered. "You'll get all the attention, and you'll look great when you congratulate him graciously from your hospital bed."

He chuckled then grimaced, tightening his fist around a wad of Chuck's jacket.

"I wish we could do more for you," Ruby said.

"They'll be here soon."

"Yeah." She looked around for Chuck, but he was out of sight. A sudden panic hit her. What if Chuck fell and injured himself, too?

"You make a cute couple," Jeff said.

She blinked in surprise. "You think?"

"Yeah." Jeff laughed. "I'm a little jealous, I admit."

She smiled, feeling a flush warm her wind-cooled cheeks.

"Chuck and I were talking about God before you came."

"Were you?" Her admiration for Chuck soared to a new high. "I'm sure God put us here with you today."

"That's pretty much what Ol' Doc said." Jeff let out a deep sigh and closed his eyes. "It's something I've pretty much put off thinking about. All the really important things. God. . . death. . .marriage."

She chuckled. "One thing at a time, Jeff."

"Yeah."

She swallowed hard and shot up a quick prayer as she considered what to say next. "Sometimes God just reaches down and grabs your attention."

"Oh, yeah. Like this." He lifted his uninjured arm in a gesture indicating his battered body.

"Yes. Like this." Ruby shut her eyes. *Lord, help us to get him out of here soon. And thank You for using this to turn Jeff's thoughts toward You.*

She pulled her cell phone from her pocket and stared bleakly at the screen. No service now. She looked up toward the trail and saw several people and horses clustered near the spot where Jeff fell. Dr. Spelling's lime-green sweater stood out. Ruby hoped the veterinarian could discourage people from dismounting and walking near the edge of the precipice. Soon several of the contestants moved on, and she let out a pent-up breath.

A scrabbling sound on the rocks drew her attention, and she turned to see Chuck hurrying back toward them. He left the rocky area and scrambled up to their level through the low brush empty-handed.

"Couldn't find anything big enough?" Ruby called.

Jeff opened his eyes and moaned.

Chuck didn't answer until he reached them and knelt beside Jeff. "How you doing, buddy?"

"About the same."

Chuck nodded. "I found something." He glanced at Ruby, his eyes glittering, and pointed back the way he'd come, into the steep-sided valley between the mountains. "It's over there, down a ways. There are trees, and it's down in a rocky ravine."

"What?" Ruby asked.

Jeff managed a weak grin. "I'll bet it's the old stagecoach."

"Nope. You'll never guess."

Ruby scowled at him. "So tell us already."

"It's a crashed airplane."

twelve

"You're kidding!" Ruby's brown eyes widened, and she stared at Chuck for a moment.

"Is it an old one?" Jeff asked. "I haven't heard of any aircraft accidents lately."

"It looks fairly recent," Chuck said. "I was poking along looking for a downed tree or something I could break into a usable length, and I saw it down below me. I didn't climb all the way down to it because I figured it would take me a while to get down there and back. There's no trail or anything."

Ruby looked down the hillside. "How big is it?"

"It looks like a Piper low-wing. Maybe a four-seater. I couldn't be sure from that distance. But it's in an area that will be hard to access. I doubt anyone would see it from above even, unless they flew in close with a chopper. That plane had to be flying low and ran right into the mountain. One of the wings is off."

Ruby seized his arm. "That could be the plane the police were waiting for Wednesday night. They staked out a private airfield, but the plane never showed."

"Where was the airstrip?"

Her brow furrowed. "Not very far from here. I think it would be on the other side of this ridge, maybe eight or ten miles away."

Chuck nodded slowly, considering that. "Could be they lost their bearings and got into the mountains without intending to."

"Wouldn't someone have known?" Jeff asked. "I mean, they'd have to file a flight plan." He winced and pulled in a ragged breath.

Ruby put her hand on his good arm. "Better not try to talk much, Jeff. But we're talking drug dealers. If they crashed, who's going to tell the authorities? They must have gotten off course and disoriented in the dark."

Chuck gulped and looked back in the direction he'd come. "There could be people in the wreckage."

"Yeah." Ruby looked intently into his eyes. "Chuck, it's been three days. If that is the plane the detectives were waiting for, it's possible there could be some injured people still down there. People have been known to live for more than a week in primitive conditions after a plane crash."

"We need to call the police," Chuck said.

Ruby nodded. "My phone won't work down here, though."

"The EMTs will be here any minute, and they'll have radios," he replied.

"Good thinking. Those detectives were so disappointed. They thought the tip they had was legitimate, and they were going to bust the drug ring that's been bringing in cocaine for a while now." Ruby bit her lip. "I hate to think there could be someone down there, dead or alive."

"It's only a slight chance." Chuck frowned as he looked out over the ravine. "But I think the fuselage is mostly intact."

"Go back and look," Jeff said. "You both feel strongly about it. Maybe you can help someone, Doc. You two go check it out."

Ruby patted Jeff's shoulder. "No, we're not going to leave you alone here."

"I'll be fine. Dr. Spelling is right up there." He nodded upward. Another knot of horses had gathered where Heather

Spelling kept her vigil. "Man, I feel bad that so many riders have lost time because of me."

Ruby pondered a moment. "Think of it this way: Chuck wouldn't have found that plane if you hadn't had your accident. Maybe some good will come of this."

"Hey, look!" Chuck pointed toward the trail. "I think the EMTs are here." He rose and waved. Dr. Spelling and several other people waved back. Chuck put his hands to his mouth and yelled, "Have them come down the way Ruby came!"

Dr. Spelling nodded and led the others back toward the easier access route.

"It won't be long now, Jeff," Ruby said. "Do you want another drink?"

"Thanks."

While they helped him sip from the canteen again, two men headed slowly down and across the slope carrying medical bags.

"Hey, Chuck!"

Chuck turned at Heather Spelling's hail from aloft.

"Yeah?"

"We're going to lower the stretcher from up here with ropes to save them from carrying it down. Can you guide it when we do?"

"Sure."

Chuck worked his way carefully up the mountainside a few yards and waited as two men lowered the stretcher. Heather stopped oncoming riders until the task was completed. After a few minutes of maneuvering, Chuck was able to reach out and steady the stretcher against the slanted ground. He was surprised to see a man fastening on a rappelling harness. By the time the climber reached Chuck, the two EMTs had also arrived.

Ruby greeted them and moved to one side to give them room to work with Jeff on the precarious hillside perch.

"How you doing, champ?" the first EMT asked.

Jeff smiled through clenched teeth. "I've been better."

They examined him and took his vital signs. In a remarkably short time they had him strapped to the stretcher. They covered him with a blanket and gave Chuck's jacket back to him.

"Thanks," Chuck said. "Need some help?"

"Thanks, but we'll get it from here," one of the EMTs said. "I think we can lift him straight up that cliff face."

Ruby squeezed Jeff's good hand. "We'll make sure Annabelle's taken care of, and I put your hat in your saddle pack."

He gave her a weak smile. "Thanks. See you later."

Several more volunteers had prepared ropes at the top of the drop-off, and soon the stretcher lifted off the ground with a climber in harness spotting.

" 'Bye, Jeff," Chuck called. He and Ruby waved as the stretcher rose. Jeff lifted his hand in farewell.

Chuck sighed and turned to the EMT. "Thanks. You guys did a great job."

"Well, it's not over yet, but you did a good job, too. Thanks for stabilizing the patient and staying with him."

"No problem." Chuck looked at Ruby. "You want to take that hike now?"

"Yes, let's, if you think we have enough daylight to get down there and back."

"It'll be a tough climb out, but yeah." Chuck turned to the EMT. "Could you make a police report for us as soon as you're topside?"

"What's up?" the EMT asked.

"I was looking for some sticks to use for splints and a makeshift stretcher, and I spotted a downed airplane."

The EMT whistled. "An old one?"

"I don't know." Chuck pointed below him and across the mountainside. "It's way down there in a ravine. The thing is, Ruby works as a dispatcher. She said the local detectives were watching for a drug dealer's plane a few nights ago, and it never came in. We're wondering if this could be the one."

"Okay, I'll call it in."

Chuck gave him as precise information as he could on the location of the plane.

"If you find any survivors, you'll need to let us know right away."

"I know," Chuck said. "I doubt there are any, but we'll do the best we can. It might take us a couple of hours to get a message out."

"Could you also ask someone to check our horses?" Ruby asked. "We might not get back up to the trail until after dark."

"Yes," Chuck said. "Maybe one of the ride officials would take them back to the nearest checkpoint where you left the ambulance. I see Tom Marden up there with Dr. Spelling, and I'm sure he'd be willing to do that."

"Anything else?" the EMT asked.

"Well, if it's not too much trouble, could I give you my dad's cell phone number?" Ruby patted her pockets then unbuckled her pack. "He and my mom are going to be waiting for me at the finish line, and they'll be awfully worried when Chuck and I don't show up. I'm sure rumors about Jeff's accident will be flying, too."

"Yeah, I think Jeff's brother will be waiting at the next rest stop," Chuck added. "Someone should tell Kevin Tavish what happened."

"Here, I have a pen. I'll make sure Jeff's brother gets the word so he can meet us at the hospital." The EMT took Ruby's father's phone number then grinned at them. "Well, you two have had yourselves quite a day. Be careful."

"We will," Chuck assured him. "Call the police first, okay?"

"Got it." He turned to climb the rugged hillside.

Chuck and Ruby watched the volunteers guide the stretcher up over the rim and onto the safety of the trail above. From there several men immediately carried it down the trail toward the checkpoint and the waiting ambulance.

Chuck let out a sigh. "Well."

"Yeah." Ruby gave him a strained smile. "Not the way we thought the afternoon would go."

Chuck nodded, studying the terrain they would have to negotiate if they went back to the plane crash site. "Listen. I've been thinking about this, and I don't think you should do it. Why don't you go on up to the trail and go on with the ride?"

She shook her head emphatically. "We've been through that."

"It's not too late to finish respectably."

"No, I want to go with you. If people are in that plane, they'll need help as soon as possible. We've got water and a few bandages and other supplies. I have a granola bar and a flashlight. Those things may make all the difference for someone. Besides, if you got hurt down there, how would I know? It would be a long time before anyone could get to you and help you." She looked at her watch. "And we're only four hours from sunset. I say let's get started."

"Okay, I can't argue with that." Her logic and determination ratcheted up his admiration for her. If he was going to venture out on a difficult mission, Ruby was the person he wanted with him. "Let me get my rope."

The climbing volunteer had unfastened the ropes Chuck used for his descent and tossed them down the slope. Chuck worked his way up to the end of the line and pulled it in. He coiled the three attached lead lines and settled the roll over his shoulder in case they needed it at the crash scene.

"Okay, let's go."

Ruby nodded with a tight smile.

Chuck worked his way slowly down and across the steep slope toward a broad, rocky area. The ground flattened out somewhat, and they were able to maneuver steadily onward, using large rocks and low bushes as support on the steeper places. When they reached a spot where the rocks fell away again in an eight-foot drop, he scooted down then turned to offer her a hand.

"Maybe you'd better drop your pack first."

She unbuckled the strap and lowered her pack into his hands then slid down the rock face.

"You okay?" Chuck extended his hand and helped her rise and steady herself.

"Yeah, I'm fine."

Chuck squeezed her hand and released it. She stooped to dust off her jeans.

The next part was easier, and for a few minutes he imagined they were out together on a pleasure hike. Sunshine, wide-open spaces, and Ruby. He looked back at her and smiled as she scrambled over a patch of scattered boulders. Before the day was over he would ask her for a real date—a time when they were in no danger of breaking their necks. No pressure from competition. No possibility lives depended on them.

He paused on a jagged boulder and reached to assist her. When she stood beside him on the rock, he pointed.

"See it?" The slash of white that was the fuselage lay at the base of a dark rock face among scrub evergreen trees at the bottom of the ravine.

She sucked in a breath. "Wow. Yeah. That's going to take some climbing."

"Want to go back?"

She shook her head and looked into his eyes. "We can do it. I'll let you lead."

"Right. Just try your cell phone again." He shaded his eyes and looked back but could no longer see the trail above or the spot where Jeff had landed when he fell. "You could never get a horse in here."

"Nope." She pushed a few buttons and held the phone to her ear. "Not ringing." She lowered it and squinted at the screen. "No good. We'd better get going."

Twenty minutes later they stood panting above the mangled plane. Now that they were close, Chuck eyed it critically, from nose to shattered tail.

"Piper Archer, I think."

"I don't know much about planes," Ruby admitted.

Its crushed nose and propeller confirmed the theory that the little plane had slammed into the cliff face. Pieces of debris gleamed amid the dull rocks. The crumpled white fuselage, too bright among the dark neutrals of the canyon, rested with the pilot's side facing him. The windows were shattered, and the near wing of the four-seat plane had sheared off on impact. Chuck hoped the other was intact so he could climb up to the cabin door. The tail and rear portion of the fuselage were squashed and battered. "No way could anyone survive that."

She grimaced. "I'm afraid you're right, but we have to be sure."

"Yes."

"So how do you get in? I don't see a door."

Chuck squinted down at the plane again. "It's on the other side above the wing. You climb up on the wing to get in. But there's a step to help you. Looks from here like the right wing may be still in place."

She looked around then glanced at him. "We're not very close to where we saw those riders yesterday."

"It's got to be a couple of miles as the crow flies," he agreed. "From where they left their horses. . .well, I can't speculate on whether they could have hiked in this far or not. I'm guessing if they were looking for this plane they didn't find it."

"We can't be sure of that." She inhaled deeply. "Ready? That last descent looks pretty rugged."

"Yeah, let me go first."

Chuck edged down the slope, groping for handholds on the rocks.

They approached cautiously, and he reached to help her several times over rough spots. When they were only a few yards from the plane, he paused.

"Let me take a look, all right? I'll call to you if it's okay."

She nodded, saying nothing, but her dark eyes searched his face.

"Could be the plane is empty," he reminded her. "This could have happened a year ago." But he knew she was thinking it couldn't be that old. The broken limbs on the trees looked fresh. And if it was an older wreck she would have heard about it through her job at the police station. Still, it made him feel better for them both to think it was so. He had to go to the broken window on the pilot's side and look in. As he turned and scrambled down to the side of the cockpit, he steeled himself for what he might find. He glanced back to make sure Ruby waited on the rock above him.

Motion beside Ruby drew his attention and stopped him cold. A man stood up in the low brush near her. Chuck's heart lurched, and he opened his mouth to yell to her. Beside him a chilly voice said sternly, "Quiet now. Back away from the plane."

Chuck turned slowly. All he needed to convince him to obey was the glint of the lowering sun on the barrel of the pistol the stranger held.

thirteen

Ruby flinched as the man behind her spoke. She didn't dare turn to look at him. Her heart rate accelerated, and blood rushed to her temples. Below her, the second man forced Chuck to move away from the crumpled plane. Chuck tripped and stumbled on the uneven ground. She wanted to scream, but the touch of something hard to her spine, just below where her small pack rested between her shoulders, silenced her.

"That's it. Don't move."

She straightened, raising her shoulders a fraction of an inch, easing away from the feel of metal against her back, but the gun barrel—she was sure it must be a gun barrel—followed, pressing even harder against her sweatshirt and her vertebrae.

"Easy now." His voice was calm, reasonable, even gentle. She swallowed hard against the saliva that flooded her mouth.

Chuck had risen and stepped cautiously toward her on the trackless hillside, hopping from rock to rock, pausing after each step to gauge the best place to put his foot down next. Close behind him came a man with dark hair showing around the edges of his gray Stetson. His faded jeans looked about to give way at one worn knee, but his long-sleeved fleece shirt, topped by a quilted black vest, looked warm and serviceable. His lined face bespoke years in the outdoors. If she'd met him on the trail, Ruby reflected, she would have smiled and passed the time of day with him. Assuming, of course, he wasn't holding that gun.

When Chuck was only a dozen feet from Ruby, below her and to her left, the man behind her spoke loudly enough for all four of them to hear.

"What now?"

His partner looked up and arched his eyebrows. His tanned face wrinkled as he looked her over. At last he spoke. "Tie them up."

The man behind Ruby moved, sending the muzzle of his gun jarring against her spine. "What good will that do? They'll blab as soon as they get free or someone finds them."

The man below frowned at him. "What were you thinking then?"

"Shoot 'em both."

Ruby sucked in a breath and looked down at Chuck. In his deep blue eyes she read sorrow and regret that he'd led her into this situation. She tried to reassure him, using only her expression. God was with them. No matter how this turned out, they would be all right. In her heart she knew it was true. Still, her logical mind laid out several possibilities, and none of them was good. She gasped for the air that seemed to have thinned.

Dear Lord, she prayed, *get us out of this. Or. . .*

She couldn't finish the thought so ended merely with, *Do what is best, dear God. Only You know what that is.*

"No one would find them for years," the blond man said. "It would be easy to hide them here."

The man with Chuck let out a sharp breath. "You're a fool. There are people within sound of a gunshot. Some of those riders on the trail up yonder would hear."

Chuck glanced toward the side, not quite turning his head toward the man. "There are people closer than that. One of the competitors in the ride was injured, and EMTs came to help him."

The man with Ruby stepped forward slightly, and she could see his profile. His hat topped long, dishwater-blond hair, and a beard filled out his narrow face. "You telling it straight?" He fixed Chuck with a defiant glare.

"Yes, sir," said Chuck. "The rider fell down the rock face not too far from here. I'm sure they'd hear it if you fired a weapon."

The two gunmen locked gazes. "Come on," said the older man from his place near Chuck. "Let's tie these two up and do what we gotta do."

The blond man threw a sidelong glance at Ruby. "That'll take time."

Ruby gulped in a breath and said, "We asked them to call the police."

The dead silence lasted a good three seconds.

"And why would you do something as helpful as that?" the older man asked, glaring up at Ruby.

Suddenly she recognized him. He was the man who'd driven the gray pickup away from the fire early this morning. Did he know she was the one who had seen him then? She swallowed hard and looked to Chuck. Had she already revealed too much? Perhaps it would have been better to keep that tidbit about the police to herself.

Chuck turned toward the gunman. "I spotted the plane wreckage when we went down the cliff to help the injured rider. I couldn't tell if it was an old one or a more recent crash, so we asked the EMTs who came to radio in and tell the police. We thought there might possibly be someone in the wreck who needed help. That's why we came over here with water and medical supplies."

"Oh, Mannie doesn't need any help," the blond man behind Ruby said with a snigger.

"Shut up," his partner snapped. "Let's get this over with. The cowboy here has a rope. You can use it to tie them up." He looked around and gestured to a tree near the broken tail of the Piper. "Put 'em over there. They'll be out of the way while we get the stuff."

Chuck's eyebrows shot up. Ruby wondered, too. What kind of *stuff*?

"Come on, little lady." The blond man prodded her with an object she was sure could fire at least six rounds and swap out an empty clip for a full one in a matter of seconds. He pushed her slightly toward the drop Chuck had negotiated earlier, and she scuttled down, sliding the last few feet and landing in a heap.

Chuck reached to help her up, but the older gunman nudged him.

"Leave her be, cowboy. She's not hurt."

Ruby rose, ignoring the minor pain in the wrist she'd scraped on the way down. The blond man hopped down beside her and steadied himself.

"Come on." He herded them toward the tree his partner had indicated. "Give me your pack."

Ruby eased the straps off over her arms and handed it to him. He opened it and rummaged through the contents, tossing a few packages of sterile dressings out on the ground. He tucked her granola bar into his pocket.

"All right, sit."

Ruby sat down, shoving aside the low branches. Chuck touched her hand just for an instant then drew away, but it was enough to encourage her. They *would* survive this.

With some difficulty their captor secured them both by

making them put their hands behind them and tying them to the tree trunk.

Meanwhile the older man approached the debris of the airplane, flinging branches and pieces of the plane out of his way.

The blond man stood back and eyed his restraining job critically. "Okay. Don't try anything, will ya?"

Ruby said nothing, and Chuck also ignored the question. The man moved away, turned his back and pushed his way through the brush toward his partner.

"You okay?" Chuck asked softly.

"Yeah." Ruby squirmed until she could see him from the corner of her eye. "Where did they come from?"

"They must have been down here and heard us coming. The one guy—the older one—was behind the wing of the plane, I think. His friend was waiting over there." Chuck nodded toward a thick stand of scrub cedars. "He got behind you after you passed him."

"They must be looking for drugs in the plane."

"That's what I figure. And they haven't found them yet, or they wouldn't have showed themselves to us."

"Maybe they fell out when the plane crashed." Ruby sighed and looked up at the blue sky. Why did such a beautiful day turn out so wrong? First the fire. That was bad enough, but then Jeff's terrifying accident. Now this. "Are they going to kill us?" she whispered.

"I don't think so."

"I should have kept my mouth shut about the police."

"Maybe not. It got their attention. It'll make them work faster. And maybe it influenced them not to fire a gun."

"I suppose so." She ran over what she knew about sentencing for criminal activity. "If they get caught looting the plane they can claim they stumbled on it, like we did."

"Right," Chuck said. "But if they get caught standing over two bodies it will be mighty hard to talk their way out of that."

The older man called from the far side of the plane, "Get over here, Jack!" The bearded, blond man hurried to his side.

Ruby strained her ears to hear what they said, but much of their conversation was too quiet for her to understand. After a moment the older man raised his chin and said, more loudly, "Oh, come on! You're smaller than I am."

"Uh-uh," said Jack. "What if I get stuck in there?"

Behind the wreck their voices continued, more muffled. The remains of the small plane shuddered. After a few minutes the big man said clearly, "Can't do it."

Jack stepped carefully around the smashed tail section. The other man followed, wiping his hands on his jeans. Jack looked over toward Chuck and Ruby and said something in a guarded tone. The older man looked their way, focusing on Ruby. She shivered.

"Take it easy," Chuck whispered.

"I'm scared."

"Of course you are. But God is with us."

She swallowed down the lump in her throat. "Thanks. But they're talking about me."

"I think you're right." Chuck strained at the rope and leaned toward her. She felt his elbow barely touch her upper arm. "Ruby, be strong. No matter what happens, God will take care of you."

She tried to respond, but her mouth went dry, and she trembled uncontrollably as Jack strode toward them through the brush. A sudden picture of her parents waiting for her at the finish line came vividly to mind. She saw the stark agony in their eyes once more—the same expression her dad's face surely held when they'd learned Julie was dead. And Mom. Could Mom take another tragedy? *God, help us.*

Chuck struggled against the rope, and it pulled Ruby's hands against the rough bark of the cedar. She sucked in her breath and held it, not watching the man coming toward her.

His shadow blocked the sun above her.

"We need you." He holstered his pistol and knelt beside her. "Now don't you do anything stupid, cowboy," he said to Chuck as he worked at the knots. "You hear me?" He paused and cocked his head to one side, glaring past Ruby at Chuck.

"I hear you." Chuck's voice was tight, and Ruby could feel his tension. "What are you going to do?"

"We just need the princess here to fetch something for us. The plane's pretty well squashed, and the cargo hold is ripped open in the back. My buddy and I can't quite get to what we want out of there."

"Don't you hurt her," Chuck said.

Jack laughed. "Or what, big guy? You'll beat me to a pulp? I don't think so."

The knots gave way, and the rope relaxed. Ruby pulled her hands around in front of her and massaged her wrists. The scrape the rocks had given her smarted and oozed blood. Jack immediately began to retie the rope. Chuck grunted, and she turned to watch. Jack seemed to enjoy pulling the rope tighter now that he had only one prisoner to restrain.

"You'll cut off his circulation," she said.

Jack smiled up at her. She couldn't control a tremble, and she hated that he saw it.

"Well, princess, I guess you'll just have to hurry if you don't want his poor little hands to go numb, won't you?"

Ruby looked down into Chuck's eyes. There were so many

things she wanted to tell him before she left his side. But Jack's presence and his snarl as he drew his gun again kept her from saying anything.

"Get moving. Thanks to you, we need to hurry." He nudged her ribs with the gun barrel. Ruby turned toward the aircraft and worked her way around it. She stepped cautiously over a strip of jagged metal and eased sideways between the side of the fuselage and a clump of brush.

The older man waited, glowering at her as she approached. Beyond him the windows on this side of the cockpit were cracked and shattered, too. The door above the wing was open. Ruby caught a glimpse of dark fabric, and her stomach roiled. She avoided looking up toward the door. Instead she focused on the man's face. Definitely the man fleeing the fire this morning.

He nodded toward a smaller open door behind the wing and gestured to it as if ushering her to a choice seat in the theater.

"There you go. Just slide on in and bring out any bags you find."

"Bags?" Ruby eyed him doubtfully. "You mean like a grocery sack?"

"No, like a gym bag. You know. A carry-on or a duffel bag." He pushed his hat back and wiped his forehead. "Come on now. Get in there."

She squatted and looked into the small opening. The framework had buckled, and torn metal hung down into the belly of the fuselage. She glanced forward. A wall separated this bay from the passenger compartment. Though it was partially collapsed, she couldn't see into the cockpit. She was glad.

"I'm not sure I can fit in there." She looked up at him.

He jerked his arm forward and pressed the muzzle of his pistol to her temple. "Sure you can."

She caught her breath and poked her head inside the small cargo bay. It had been no bigger than the trunk of a car originally, but in the wreck the rear dividers had torn free. She could see daylight through holes in back of the compartment.

"I don't see anything."

Jack swore. "Just get in there and take a look."

"That's right." The older man gestured with his gun toward the rear of the plane. "I thought I saw something stuck back there, but I couldn't reach it. I figure when the plane hit and fell, the bags shifted. Now get in there and see if you can get 'em."

Ruby pulled in a shaky breath and eyed a sharp piece of metal protruding from the side of the craft inside the compartment.

Behind her, the older man said to his partner, "Did you tie the cowboy up good?"

"Oh, yeah," said Jack.

"Wouldn't want him getting loose now."

"No, we wouldn't."

Ruby leaned forward and crawled inside. She lay on her side and slithered around the jagged metal. Behind the luggage compartment the smashed top of the tail section bowed down to within a foot of the bottom. She swallowed hard. The stench of fuel overrode the clean smell of cedar, and another smell—faint but foul—teased her nostrils. She scrunched her face up and inched forward, looking for luggage. The scrape on her wrist hurt, but she ignored it.

Ahead of her she saw something dark, wedged between broken members of the framework. She reached toward it, but it was just beyond her grasp.

"Find anything?" one of the men yelled. He sounded far

away, as if he were talking through a toy tin can "telephone" like she and Julie used to make when they were kids.

"There's something, but I can't reach it."

"Try harder, princess."

She swallowed down the bitter taste in her mouth and squeezed forward. Her head wouldn't fit beneath the bent metal of the aluminum frame without her forcing it. What if she got stuck? Would Jack grab her feet and pull her out? Or would they go off and leave her here?

"I can't."

The older man's voice came, louder and more distinct. "You'd better. Because we have no reason to keep your friend alive. If you like him, get whatever bags you find and haul them out here. Fast."

She gritted her teeth and blinked back tears, praying desperately in the silence. She shoved her shoulder against the broken metal. It gave slightly, and her outstretched fingers touched the dark fabric. Nylon? More like canvas. It certainly felt like a duffel bag.

She relaxed for a moment, panting.

"Whatcha got?" Jack yelled.

"There's some kind of cloth item. It could be a bag. But I can't get it free. Do you have any tools?" Her voice sounded close and tinny.

A low murmuring behind her was all she could make out of the men's conversation. Louder came the sigh of the wind through the canyon, making the loose edges of the wreckage quiver.

The walls of fractured metal pressed in on her. *It's okay*, she told herself. *It's like an MRI machine.*

Her heart raced, and the air she gulped didn't seem to fill her lungs. She couldn't stand the closeness any longer. She had to know she could free herself. Inching backward, she scuffed her knees on the metal ribs and slid along the floor.

"Hey!" the older man shouted. "Did you get it?"

She kept going. At last her left foot found the edge of the opening to the side. She wriggled out and sat gasping on the ground.

"Where's the bag?" Jack loomed over her.

She turned her face away. "I told you, I can't get it. There's too much trash in the way. You'll need tools. Metal cutters."

"Well, darlin', we don't have any tools," the older man said. "So just make up your mind to go back in there."

"No."

Jack raised his pistol over his head and swung his arm back, as though he would strike her with it. His partner caught his wrist.

"Hold on there. If you beat her up she won't be any use to us."

Jack's scowl suddenly brightened. "The cowboy."

Ruby and the other man looked at him.

Jack shrugged. "He's big and strong."

Both men walked to the back of the plane and looked toward Chuck. Ruby stood shakily and followed.

"Think you can help us?" the older man called.

"I'm willing to try." Chuck leaned forward, pulling at the rope that bound him. His gaze locked on Ruby for a moment. She tried to smile, but tears were so close she could only grimace and sniff.

"You think we'd trust you, cowboy?" Jack yelled.

Chuck met the bearded man's glare with a level gaze. "I won't try anything. Just leave Ruby alone, and I'll help you tear that plane apart."

The two gunmen looked at each other. The older man

spread his hands in indecision. "I don't trust him," he muttered.

"If we wait too long, the cops will fly in here with a chopper," Jack said.

"If they really called the cops. I think she just said that to make us nervous."

They both frowned at Ruby.

"How about it, princess?" Jack leaned toward her with his hands on his thighs, his gaze drilling into her. "Did you call the cops or not?"

Suddenly her claustrophobia was worse than it had been in the plane. She turned her face away. "Yes. Not us, but we asked the EMTs to make the call. We told them we were coming down here to see if there was anyone still alive from the crash."

Jack stretched his arms and popped his elbow joints. The wind whooshed over them, and a loose piece of metal flapped against the fuselage.

"Get the cowboy," the older man said. "We need to get that stuff and get out of here."

"What if he gets tough?"

"Then we shoot him."

fourteen

Chuck held his breath as the two men conferred. Would they untie him and let him help them find what they wanted in the debris? His hands were numb, and his elbows ached from his awkward position.

Lord, let them be reasonable. Please don't let them hurt Ruby. I can deal with anything else. Just please make them leave her alone.

His stomach had churned since the moment the bearded man called Jack had come to fetch Ruby. So far they hadn't injured her, but that could change any moment. From his vantage point he couldn't see what they were doing, but it appeared they had forced her to enter the downed plane. Now Ruby was outside, and he'd heard her refuse to go in again. What horrors had she encountered in the wreckage? The haunted cast in her brown eyes moved him to promise them anything.

Jack climbed up toward Chuck again. Ruby pushed back a loose lock of her hair and followed the outlaw's progress with her eyes. Chuck refused to speculate on what would happen but focused on Ruby's pale face instead. *It's all right. God will protect us.* If only he could get that across to her.

"Hold still." Jack tussled with the knots he'd tied.

Chuck tried not to move while he worked. After a minute of failure Jack swore and pulled out a pocket knife. Chuck said nothing but made a mental note to buy Jeff a new lead rope.

"All right, move."

Chuck staggered to his feet and slapped his arms against his chest. As the burning sensation of restored blood flow hit his hands, he rubbed them vigorously.

"I said move," Jack snarled.

Chuck stumbled toward where Ruby and the other man waited by the plane.

"Come on," the older man said. "We've had good luck until this week. But if we get caught here we're looking at some serious time in the hoosegow. Let's get this done."

Ruby pressed her lips together.

Jack eyed Chuck with speculation. "Your girlfriend's scared to go in there again."

"It's too close." Her voice broke. "There is something in there—maybe the bag they want—but I couldn't get to it. It's way in the back, behind where the baggage is supposed to be. There's metal hanging down, and I couldn't get through."

Chuck eyed the fuselage and the torn wing structure. "There's a gap on the top of the tail section. Have you looked in there to see if you can spot it?"

"Can't say as we have." The older man lifted his gray Stetson and wiped his forehead with a bandana. "You're not going to cut and run, are you?"

Chuck looked down the ravine. "Where to?"

The man nodded with a grim smile. "Right. So maybe you and Jack can clear some of the trash out of that hole from above and we can drop Miss Ruby in through the rip."

Ruby shivered and hugged herself, but Chuck shook his head. "I can tell from here the hole's not big enough. But maybe we can clear the fuselage out enough so one of us can go in." Chuck watched his captors' expressions but saw no enthusiasm.

"That would take too long," Jack said. "Let's just rip off

some more metal and stuff her in there."

Chuck wished he could touch Ruby, just a simple squeeze of the hand to reassure her, but Jack stood between them and clearly expected him to climb up on the plane's tail and start working.

"Where's the backpack we had?" Chuck asked. "We had a flashlight. That might be useful."

Jack flailed about in the brush and came up with the red backpack. He tossed it to Ruby. She opened the front flap and extracted a small flashlight.

"All right, let's do this," Jack said. "You coming, Hap?"

His partner shrugged. "One of us had better watch the princess, don't you think?"

"Oh, right, and that just naturally has to be you." Jack swore under his breath and followed Chuck.

Chuck tested his weight against the buckled framework on the right side of the fuselage and climbed up, straddling the tail section the way he would a horse. He slid forward to where he could peer in through the yawning hole. He looked down at Jack, who stood on the ground below him.

"Do you think the baggage is clear at the back?" Logic told him it would have shifted forward on impact; but if the plane tilted or spun when it fell, anything was possible.

Jack scratched his chin through his beard. "It shoulda been in the hold right behind the seats, but it could have shifted anywhere. The gal said she saw something in the tail, but I suppose it could even have fallen out someplace over the mountains."

Chuck shook his head. "Most of the plane is right here, and the worst breach is high. I'm betting your cargo is still inside. But getting at it may take some doing."

"Well, make it snappy."

Chuck looked around. "Get me a branch or a long piece of debris. Something sturdy and long enough to reach down in there. Maybe I can pry things apart enough for you or Ruby to get farther back in there."

"Not me." Jack shuffled into the brush and picked up a piece of metal Chuck hazarded to be part of an aileron. He flexed it in his hands.

"Too flimsy," Chuck called. "I need to be able to push and pry with it."

Jack turned to a small pine that had been flattened by the plane. "Maybe I can break the branches off this."

While he waited, Chuck leaned down into the fuselage and moved some wires out of the way. He was also able to reach pieces of the jumbled debris inside but couldn't tell if he was making headway in the retrieval mission. At last Jack brought him a five-foot stick with stubs of limbs sticking out down its length.

"Guess it will have to do." Chuck hefted it and poked the fatter end into the hole. Bracing it against the edge of the gap for leverage, he pushed on the broken metal inside the plane. It gave and folded toward the wall. He strained to push out the caved-in aluminum walls. After several minutes he felt he'd made enough changes that a small person might be able to squeeze past the trash that had stopped Ruby earlier.

"Okay," he told Jack. "Go around to the door and see if you can get in there."

"Not me," Jack said again.

Chuck scowled at him. Ruby was the only one of them smaller than Jack. Looking across the top of the Piper, he could see the older man, Hap. Ruby must be sitting near him in the shadow of the airplane.

"Ruby," he called.

She stood and stepped away from the plane, beside Hap, and gazed up at Chuck. The sun was long beyond the mountains, and twilight was snaking into the canyon, but even in the shadows her pallor struck him.

"Do you think you can try again? I've pried some of the pieces of metal to one side."

She swallowed hard. "I. . .guess so."

"I'll be right here. Give it a go. I think I'll be able to see you once you get in a few feet, past that luggage compartment."

She nodded. "Are you praying?"

"Yes." He was surprised she'd said it aloud. Hap's eyes narrowed, but he made no comment. Ruby adjusted the visor of her baseball cap and disappeared from view. A few seconds later he heard muffled sounds from within the plane, soft thuds and a creak. The whole thing shook. Chuck put his face to the hole again. A moment later he saw her hand fumbling among the wreckage.

"Hey! I see your hand. You okay?"

"Yeah. I can't see you."

He stuck his arm through the gaping hole and waved. "How about now?"

"Oh, yeah."

"Do you see the bags they want?"

"I'm not sure. There's something about a yard ahead of me. I may be able to reach it this time."

Chuck could hear her strained breathing as she worked her way farther into the tail of the plane. Her cap appeared below him in the shadows as she worked laboriously onward.

"You can do it," he said softly. "If it's what they want they may leave us alone after you get it for them."

She stopped moving. "What if they don't?"

Her dread washed over him, and he wished he could assure

her the men wouldn't hurt them, but anything could happen at this point. "Keep praying."

"Hey, quit yakking!" Jack yelled. "We need to get out of here."

Chuck turned and looked down at him. "She's doing her best. Just take it easy."

"Chuck!"

Ruby's faint call snagged his attention, and he put his face back to the tear in the metal, shading his eyes so he could see better. The beam of her small flashlight showed him her head and arms in the tight enclosure.

"I'm here, Ruby. What is it?"

"I think I have what they want. It's a travel bag."

"Will it fit through this hole?"

"I don't think so. And I don't think I could get it up there anyway. There's not enough room to maneuver in here. But I have it loose, so I think I can drag it out with me."

"Right." He wished he could transfer his strength to her.

"I'm backing out now."

"I'll tell our pals." Chuck looked around for Jack. He had sat down on the ground and was watching him from beneath half-closed eyelids. "Look alive, Jack. She's coming out."

Hap had climbed onto the remaining wing and from what Chuck could see was rifling the cabin, but he heard the announcement and pulled back from the doorway.

"She find it?"

"She's got something," Chuck said. "No guarantees."

Hap jumped down off the wing and joined Jack beside the cargo door. Chuck debated whether to keep his post or not and decided he wanted to be close to Ruby when they examined her loot. If it didn't make the two men happy, he wanted to be near enough to defend her if needed.

He slid down the side of the plane's tail and landed on the ground just as Ruby's sneakers appeared at the open cargo door.

"All right, princess!" Jack leaned forward to help her climb out. When she was on the ground he reached in and pulled out a navy-blue duffel bag.

Hap grinned at his partner. "That's it."

Jack unzipped the bag and smiled. "Sure enough." He quickly examined the contents. "Good job."

"Can we go now?" Chuck asked.

Jack turned to eye him thoughtfully. "I suppose I should've said, 'Good half a job.' There's supposed to be another bag."

"Cut your losses," Chuck told him. "Be thankful you have this one."

"He may have a point," Hap said. "Those cops could be flying over any second."

"Naw, we've got to get it all." Jack zipped the bag. "We've got to buy a new plane, in case you didn't notice, and a new pilot to go with it." He turned and fixed his gaze on Ruby. "You done good, honey. Now you gotta do it one more time for Uncle Jack."

Ruby's mouth twitched. She looked down at the ground.

"Don't make her go in there again," Chuck said.

Hap drew his pistol and leveled it at him. "I'm getting sick of you, cowboy."

"No!" Ruby grabbed Hap's arm. "I'll do it. But you have to promise to let us go afterward."

Hap looked at Jack.

Jack's lips skewed in a grimace. "I'm not sure we can do that."

"Yes, you can." Ruby gulped in a breath. "We won't tell anyone. And you can leave first. We'll stay here until you have a good head start. I promise."

Jack looked at Hap, who shrugged and stuck his pistol back in his holster.

"Maybe we could just tie them up again and leave them here. Their friends would find them by morning." Hap eyed Chuck as he spoke.

Was this where he should chime in with Ruby and promise not to turn them in? Chuck knew he couldn't do that.

"They might rat on us." Jack shook his head. "I dunno. Let's see what you bring out this time, princess. If you're a good girl, I'll think about it."

Ruby took two shaky breaths, turned on her flashlight, and climbed back into the cargo bay.

Chuck climbed up onto the tail section once more and watched from above as she again crept into the belly of the plane.

"How you doing?" he asked softly as she reached the area just below him.

"I'm okay. Should we stall them or give them what they want?"

"Do you see the other bag?" The fuselage lurched, and he glanced behind him. The two gunmen had gone to the front of the plane where Hap again clambered onto the wing and leaned into the cabin.

"What was that?" Ruby's white face stared up at him.

"Hap's checking the cockpit. I don't think they can hear us right now."

"In that case, yes, there's another bag like the first one. Should I bring it out, or will that mean they don't need us anymore?"

Chuck bit his lip and drew in a breath. "Not sure. But if you don't pull it out for them they might just get angrier."

"That's what I figure."

"Ruby. . ."

She waited, looking up at him, her dark eyes huge.

"If things go bad, just remember God is in control, and. . . well, I think you're the bravest woman I ever met."

She sobbed. "Thanks. Here goes nothing." She inched ahead and lay prone, with just the back of her legs from her knees down in his view.

Chuck prayed silently and looked back. Hap was handing a small item down to Jack, who stood on the ground below the wing. Chuck put his ear to the tear in the metal again and heard Ruby panting as she struggled to retrieve the rest of the cargo. Finally she edged backward and looked up at him. She shone the beam of her flashlight on another dark travel bag.

"What do you think?"

"Let's trust God to get us out of this. Bring it out."

By the time he slid to the ground, Hap was hauling her out of the cargo bay. Jack pounced on the bag she carried.

"All right! I knew you could do it."

Hap hoisted the first bag and looped the strap over his shoulder. "Let's get out of here."

"What?" Jack stared at him. "You gonna just leave these two here? We've got to tie them up at least. You said so before."

"They did give their word," Hap said.

Chuck edged closer to Ruby, ready to step in front of her if Jack drew his gun again. He hoped Hap wouldn't recall he hadn't given his word—only Ruby had.

"Oh, excuse me," Jack said with a sneer. "Their word is golden."

"Shut up!" Hap raised his arm with fingers outspread.

"What do you—"

"Hush!" Hap glared at Jack. "Hear that? I'm telling you, we've got to move!"

Ruby raised her chin, frowning. Chuck heard it then—the distant, throbbing engine of a helicopter. Was it the state police? He didn't care. It was enough to send the two drug runners scrambling.

He watched as Jack grabbed his canteen from the grass and shouldered the second bag Ruby had found. Hap had already dodged around the tail of the Piper with the first bag.

"Adios, princess," Jack called and followed his partner.

Chuck let out a deep sigh. "Think it's the cops?"

"I don't know," Ruby said in a tight voice. "I think the nearest police chopper is in Cheyenne. Maybe it's just someone out on a sightseeing tour."

Chuck strode to the wing of the plane and climbed up. He looked into the cockpit and swallowed the bile that rose in his throat. He shut his eyes for a moment then turned and jumped down. Ruby stood silently, watching him with huge, brown eyes.

"The pilot's dead." Chuck hurried to the tail and around the back of the plane. He spotted Jack and Hap rushing down the canyon, hopping over rocks. Ruby came and stood beside him. He felt her small hand touch his and closed his fingers around hers.

"They must have their horses tied up at the mouth of the canyon," she said.

"Or a truck hidden somewhere on an old trail. Ready to hike?" he asked without looking at her.

"Yeah. Think we can make it up to the rim before dark?"

"I don't know. It'll be a rugged climb, and we don't have much daylight." He turned and eyed her carefully, speculating on how much energy she had left after the ordeal. "If you're too tired I can try to get up there and call for help while you rest."

"No. Don't leave me here alone."

The helicopter seemed to be no closer, though he could still hear its thrumming motor. He nodded. "Okay, let's go." He found the red backpack and some of the scattered packages of bandages. He put them in it and held it out to her. Ruby added her flashlight. "That may come in handy later," he said. "Let's get the lead lines."

She nodded and straightened suddenly, peering down the canyon. "The chopper's louder."

Chuck caught his breath. "Maybe they really are looking for us."

"Let's get up on that rise," Ruby said, pointing to where she'd stood when Jack and Hap first appeared. "They'll be able to see us better."

They clambered up the steep slope. When they stood on the ledge she peeled off her dark sweatshirt. Her light-colored shirt would show up better, Chuck realized. He whipped off his jacket and cotton shirt, though it was getting colder, so his white T-shirt would show. He could wave his jacket if the searchers came close.

The helicopter hovered a half mile down the canyon then resumed its approach. The engine noise grew louder, almost unbearable as the echoes crashed off the cliffs around them. Ruby clamped both hands to her ears.

"They can't land here!" Chuck yelled.

She nodded, watching the chopper as it roared above them. Its wind swept over them, and Ruby waved the sweatshirt wildly. Chuck waved, too. The chopper backed off and hovered. A man leaned out the side with a speaker horn.

"Are you Dr. Sullivan?"

"Yes!" Chuck waved his jacket.

"We can't land to pick you up, but we can drop you a

survival pack. Can you walk out?"

Chuck and Ruby waved harder.

The chopper moved in lower. A bright yellow parcel tumbled out and landed in a clump of juniper twenty yards away. Chuck and Ruby ran to it as quickly as they could. Inside were a water bottle, a small first aid kit, two protein bars, a pack of matches and a radio transmitter. Ruby grabbed the radio. Chuck was surprised at how confidently she turned it on, but he supposed that was part of her training at the police station.

The chopper moved off and beat the air a hundred yards away.

"Hello," Ruby said into the radio's microphone. "Can anyone hear me?"

"We hear you," came a strong voice. "We're with the Wyoming State Police. Are you all right?"

"Yes, we're both fine."

"Are you Ruby Dale?"

"Yes, sir. Dr. Sullivan is with me. Did you see the two men leaving here a few minutes ago?"

"We did. We have ground units searching for their vehicle."

"They may have horses," Ruby said. "They're carrying two duffel bags full of drugs from the crashed plane at the head of this canyon."

"We'll do our best to intercept them," said the man in the helicopter.

"It may be a little easier if you triangulate my cell phone and use the GPS locater in it," Ruby told him. "I stuffed it into one of the two bags of contraband they recovered."

fifteen

Ruby and Chuck scrambled up the treacherous hillside. Dusk had fallen in the canyon, and she handed Chuck her flashlight so he could spot the best footholds as he led the way higher. A half hour later Chuck stopped and turned to help her climb up beside him.

"Look there, Ruby. See that?"

On the hillside above them other lights bobbed along, slowly progressing toward them.

"It's a rescue party, looking for us." The knowledge warmed her, but at the same time sent a tinge of guilt throughout her weary body. As rescuers, she and Chuck had become the victims to be rescued, something she'd hoped to avoid. "I told the state police we were okay."

Chuck clapped her on the shoulder. "It's okay. They wanted to come help us, so let them do their thing. Imagine your folks and the riding club members wondering what had happened to us. We had all the excitement today. Let them have a little glory."

She nodded. It was true the emergency workers and volunteers who had come out to search for them would want to feel they had accomplished something, rather than staying idly at home. "Right. And I'm starved. I'll even let them give me a chocolate bar if they have one. I think Jack ate my granola bar, and those protein bars the helicopter dropped are long gone."

Just below the spot where Jeff had fetched up against a

scrub pine, stopping his fall, they met a party of three men from the local police department.

"Ahoy, Dr. Sullivan," the leader called. "Is that you, Ruby?"

Nelson Flagg's cheerful voice brought tears to her eyes. "Yeah," she yelled. "Hello, yourself, Nels!"

They sat down for a few minutes to rest, and the officers plied them with water bottles and snacks. Ruby leaned back on the hillside and sucked the chocolate coating off the candied peanuts Nels offered her while Chuck gave them a condensed version of their adventure.

"Tomorrow our detectives are going to hike in the long way from the mouth of the canyon," Flagg said. "It's too rough to try it in the dark. The state police said they saw the plane wreckage from their helicopter but can't land in there. They're preparing for an all-day expedition on foot."

"It will take them at least a couple of hours to hike in," Ruby said. "Hey, can you guys patch through to my dad's phone on the radio somehow?"

"We can be up on the trail in ten minutes," Officer Chet Baker said. "You can call him from there."

She shook her head. "I'm afraid my cell phone is either evidence by now, or else it's been ditched and I'll never see it again."

"How's that?" Flagg asked.

Ruby looked up at Chuck. All she wanted right now was her own bed and about ten hours' sleep.

Chuck smiled at her. "Ruby's about the quickest-thinking woman I know. Not only did she report the fire quickly this morning, but she also thought of a way for the police to track the drug dealers."

The men all looked at Ruby. "What did you do?"

"Not much. I just put my cell phone into the last bag of

drugs they made me take out of the plane. If the state police trace it they may be able to follow those men wherever they go. On the other hand, if my dad tries to call me and the crooks discover it early on they'll probably toss it into some place that would be hard to get at, and the police will be on a wild goose chase."

They waited while Flagg radioed in a request to notify her father. A few minutes later he told Ruby, "Your folks will be waiting at the Bear Creek clearing where the endurance ride officials had the last checkpoint you visited. We can call them by phone as soon as we get back up onto the trail. Oh, and I warned them not to try to call your cell phone."

"Sound good?" Chuck asked her, smiling.

"Very good."

"Your horses were led back to the checkpoint, too," Flagg added. "Jeff Tavish's horse went back with one of the other veterinarians—Dr. Spelling. She was going to make sure his brother and friends took it home."

"Great," Ruby said. "They'll take good care of Annabelle until Jeff recovers."

A contingent of volunteer searchers joined them, and they were soon climbing up the steep hillside to the trail. Full darkness had descended, and the moon rose to the east, among the myriad stars. Every muscle in Ruby's body screamed with fatigue, but she made herself continue plodding upward, sometimes bent over and grasping at the scant bushes for support, sometimes clutching one of the volunteers' hands. When they at last reached the edge of the path and strong hands pulled her up onto the trail where she and Chuck had ridden with Jeff, she staggered and reached for the nearest arm to steady her.

A warm arm slipped around her waist, and Chuck said in

her ear, "Are you okay?"

She leaned against him for an instant then pulled in a big breath. "Yes, I'm fine. Just tired."

"We can rest here if you need to."

She shook her head and pulled away. "It's tempting, but I'm afraid if I sit down again tonight I'll never get up."

"Miss Dale!" Fire Chief Ripton strode toward her, shining a powerful flashlight on the ground. "We have a couple of four-wheelers here. They aren't normally allowed on this trail, but we thought you and Dr. Sullivan might be glad to have a ride down to the Bear Creek clearing. Your parents and Dr. Hogan are waiting for you there."

Ruby let her shoulders sag and laid her hand on his sleeve. "Thank you, Chief. That sounds wonderful."

The ride to the checkpoint passed in a blur. Ruby leaned against the back of the firefighter driving the four-wheeler and dozed. When they reached the clearing she climbed stiffly off the vehicle and fell into her mother's arms.

"Baby, we were so worried," her mom murmured.

Tears filled Ruby's eyes. Her parents must have relived the hours after Julie's accident. She pulled them both into a big hug. "Mom, Dad, I'm okay. Honest."

Her father sobbed, and Ruby's tears spilled over.

They stood for a long moment together; then she eased gently away. "Is Lancelot okay?"

"He's great," her father said. "I've got him hitched to the trailer, and Dr. Hogan has Chuck's Appy. Are you sure you're all right? The policeman who spoke to us last said something about a plane crash."

"I'll tell you all about it on the way home." As she turned toward the parking area, she saw ride volunteers were dismantling the check-in and veterinary exam areas. "Are all the riders past this point?" she asked.

Her father nodded. "Doc Hogan told me the last of the contestants passed through here about a half hour ago."

Ruby looked around and saw Chuck had walked over to Dr. Hogan's truck and was deep in conversation with his partner.

"Ruby?"

She pivoted. Officers Flagg and Baker approached her and her parents.

"What's up?" she asked.

"We just got word the state police arrested two men loading horses into a trailer near the main road," Flagg said. "Your cell phone trick worked."

She smiled up at him. "I'm glad. Tell me, was their trailer hitched to a light-colored pickup? Because I forgot to mention that one of the men who kidnapped Chuck and me was the same man I saw early this morning at the site of the fire."

"Really?" Flagg asked. "I'm not sure about the truck. But it's late, and I think you've had enough excitement for one day. You can go home and rest and then come down to the station in the morning to identify the prisoners."

"Thanks. I think I'll do that." She realized Chuck had come over and was standing at her elbow as she said good night to the officers.

"Are you all set, Ruby?" he asked. "I guess your folks will want to baby you tonight."

"No doubt."

Chuck nodded with a smile. "Would you mind if I came by in the morning and took you to the police station? I know you go there all the time, but they want me to identify Jack and Hap, too. I was thinking we could ride over together in my pickup. Maybe get some coffee afterward."

"I'd like that."

He nodded. "Good night then. I'll pick you up around eight." He walked toward Dr. Hogan's truck.

"Hey," she called after him.

He turned back and arched his eyebrows.

"We did great on the first half of the ride."

He grinned. "We sure did. And there's a fifty-miler up near Sheridan next spring. You want to train for it?"

Ruby smiled. "I'll give that my consideration when I'm not about to fall asleep on my feet."

He strode back to her side and leaned close. "Consider this, too, would you? I think you're terrific. There's no one I'd rather have spent the day with, even a day as lousy as today." He stooped and kissed her cheek then backed away.

Her father ambled over. "Ready to go? I've got Lancelot loaded. You can ride with Mother, and I'll haul the trailer."

"Thanks, Dad." Ruby slipped her hand into his and walked with him toward where her mom waited beside the Jeep.

❧

"Hey, Ruby. Dr. Sullivan. Thanks for dropping by." Detective Garrett Austin sank into the chair opposite them in his office at the police station.

Chuck leaned back and watched Austin as he shuffled a few files on his desktop, selected one, and opened it. A week had passed since the Wyoming 100, but it seemed far longer.

"Just wanted to update you both, since you discovered the drug dealers' wrecked plane and were instrumental in us catching two of the gang members."

"Thanks, Garrett," Ruby said. "We've wondered what's going on with Jack and Hap."

Austin scrutinized the papers in the folder. "Well, they've admitted they were out looking for the downed plane the day before the ride."

"That's when we saw them the first time," Ruby said.

Chuck leaned forward. "Right. The day we posted the trail markers, and they left their horses tied up in the woods for hours."

Austin nodded. "Yes. Hap cracked first, hoping for a lighter sentence, and when Jack knew his buddy had talked he sang, too. They knew about the cocaine in the plane, and they were desperate to find it before anyone else did. They located it, but it was too late to get down to it before dark and retrieve the drugs. They decided to come back on Saturday. You saw them when they had left the canyon and gone back to where they'd tied their mounts."

"But Saturday was the ride," Ruby said.

"That's right. Jack told us they saw a poster for the Wyoming 100 and realized on Saturday and Sunday a lot of people would be riding through the area and they would risk being seen again."

"So why didn't they wait until Monday?" Chuck asked. "Why take the risk of hiking all the way in there during the ride?"

Austin leaned back in his chair and smiled. "Because Monday was the opening day of elk hunting season. There would be hunters everywhere, even where there were no trails. Someone else might see them in the canyon or, worse yet, find the plane before they could get to it."

Ruby's eyes narrowed as she listened. "So that's why they set the fire at the starting area."

"Yes, they hoped to stop the ride. That would give them the weekend pretty much to themselves to get the job done."

"But that didn't work," Chuck said, "thanks to Ruby's showing up early. The damage was minimal, and the ride went on pretty much as planned. So they took the chance of being seen during the ride and tried to recover the drugs."

"Right. You two stumbled upon them when you climbed down to check the wreckage for survivors." Austin leveled his gaze at Ruby. "You were lucky to get out of that one alive. You know that, don't you?"

"God protected us," she said.

Chuck smiled. "She's right. I prayed constantly during the hour we spent with those guys. God was merciful and allowed us to walk out with only a few scrapes and bug bites."

"Well, someone was looking out for you all right." Austin tapped the papers on his desk to align them and put them back in the folder. "Oh, and you got your cell phone back, right?"

Ruby smiled and pulled it from her purse. "It's right here. The state police brought it back a couple of days ago."

"Good. That thing led them right to the suspects."

"I'm glad. I was afraid it would ring and the two crooks would find it before the police found them. Even though I couldn't get a signal down in the canyon, I left it on, hoping it would get within range of a tower or two so the police could track it. I knew it was a risk. If someone had called me while they were carrying it and the signal had gone through. . . well, I guess the worst they could have done was to smash it or throw it away." She shook her head. "It never occurred to me to set it on vibrate instead of ring. Maybe next time. . ."

"Let's hope there won't be a next time," Chuck said.

"It's a good thing it didn't ring while they were with you." Austin shook his head. "Guess you were pretty sure it wouldn't while you were down there near the plane. But still. Those guys have assault records. They might have gotten violent if they knew you were setting them up."

"So what about the drug suppliers up the line?" Chuck asked.

The detective inhaled briskly. "Yeah, we think we may get

a break there. Harold Smith, the man called 'Hap,' gave us a couple of names. Their pilot was flying the cocaine in from Texas where they have a contact with a supplier over the border. This bust may go a long way toward stopping the flow of drugs into Wyoming, at least for a while."

Ruby smiled. "Then it was worth it."

When they left the police station, Chuck opened the door of his pickup for her. Ruby climbed up, holding her skirt expertly out of the way. She seemed as much at ease in her Sunday outfit as she had in her jeans and sweatshirt. With her hair pinned up in the back, she looked older and more pensive. He went around to the driver's side and got in.

"How are we doing for time?" Ruby asked.

"I think Sunday school is over, but we have plenty of time to meet your parents at your church before the worship service starts."

"Sounds good. Thanks. I wouldn't have minded going to your church today, but my folks are still in the smothery mood, and Grandma Margaret is there, too."

"It's all right." Chuck reached over and squeezed her hand. It was definitely all right. "They just need a little time to unwind and realize you're not going to leave them suddenly, like Julie did."

She nodded in silence, and he wondered if he'd said too much. Her eyes glistened as she looked up at him. "Thank you. I'm glad you understand. I don't think they'll be this way forever. In fact, I was talking to them last week about the possibility of getting my own place soon."

"What did they say?"

Ruby shrugged. "They're not crazy about it. I told them I wouldn't go far unless I found a place with a barn for Lancelot. Of course, Dad said, 'Why bother if you're going to be over here all the time to ride the horse anyway?' But I can't just live with them forever. I love them, but I need to have my own life."

Chuck put his key in the ignition. "I'll pray about that, if you don't mind."

"Would you? Because sometimes I feel like I can't breathe when I'm around them."

After church, as they gathered their things, Chuck said, "How would you like to go out to the steakhouse for dinner? Then I could show you my place."

"Well, I—"

"Oh, Ruby," her mother said, "you've got to eat with us today. Of course Chuck's invited, too."

"Now, Linda," Martin began.

His wife set her jaw. "Grandma and Elsie are leaving tomorrow. It'll be Ruby's last chance to see them for a while."

Chuck looked helplessly at Ruby, trying to discern her true feelings. She smiled and turned to her mother.

"Okay, Mom. But Chuck and I are taking a ride afterward. He wants to show me where his ranch is."

"You have a ranch, Doc?" Martin asked.

Chuck smiled sheepishly. "It's a very small ranch, sir. Only ten acres and a very small house. But that's good. If it were any bigger I probably couldn't handle it on my own."

"Well, that's nice." Martin eyed him as if about to say more but clamped his lips together. He took his wife's arm. "Come on, Linda. Let's go get dinner ready. The kids have places to go this afternoon."

❧

Late in the afternoon Ruby called the hospital on her cell phone as Chuck drove them down the county road in his truck.

"Hi, Ruby," came Jeff's voice, more cheerful than it had been all week.

"Hey, champ! How are you doing?"

He laughed. "Better. I'm going home tomorrow."

"That so?" she asked.

"Yeah. I'm getting around really well on my crutches."

"How's the arm?"

"Still hurts like crazy, but since they put the pin in they say it'll heal completely. I won't have full use back for a while, though. I'll be going to physical therapy for at least three months."

"Chuck asked me to tell you he'd come see you tomorrow. But if you're going home. . ."

"Tell him not to do that. I'll be gone for sure. But I'll drive down and see you both in a few weeks, as soon as they clear me to drive on my own."

"That would be great, Jeff. How's Annabelle doing?"

"Kevin and Kaye are spoiling her. But it's all right. They've decided to get married, so I won't hold it against them. I'll have Kev back on the ranch full-time again."

"That's terrific. Will they be living with you?"

"I'm thinking of giving them the ranch house and building a kit log cabin down in the back field," Jeff said.

"Sounds like a plan. Keep us posted, will you?"

"Sure will. Say hi to the doc for me."

Ruby told Chuck the gist of the conversation and sat back in contentment as he drove the pickup onto a butte. She knew they were close to his home. She was curious about it, but she didn't say anything. She wanted to see it the way he wanted to present it.

He slowed and pulled the truck onto a gravel spot beside the road. He smiled over at her then climbed out and walked around to open her door for her.

Ruby hopped down, glad she'd changed her dress shoes for her loafers. They walked to a low fence at the edge of the butte and looked out over the plain.

"See that place down there? The one with the green roof?" Chuck pointed to a ranch almost directly beneath them.

Ruby swallowed hard before she spoke. The house was tiny, and the attached barn leaned toward the sunset. A few pieces of rusty farm equipment sat about the yard, and even from a distance she could see the yard wasn't well kept.

"I see it."

"Well, count over two houses. That one's mine." He nodded westward.

She caught her breath. "The one with the creek?"

"Yup. The stream flows right through my pasture."

She stood motionless, taking in the neat dooryard, the compact but inviting house, and the barn that stood a few yards away near the fence line.

"Oh, there's Rascal," she said. The Appaloosa grazed contentedly in the field.

"Yeah, he loves it out there. See the stand of trees at the far end of the pasture? He goes down there when it's hot."

"Ten acres?"

"That's right." He looked down at her, his brows arched in question.

"I like it."

Chuck smiled and slid his arm around her shoulders. "You know, if we're going to do that fifty-mile ride in the spring we need to keep the horses in shape."

"Sure. I plan to ride as much as I can. Until we get snow anyway."

He pulled her a little closer. "Since we did so well on the

first half of the Wyoming 100, we ought to excel at doing a fifty-miler." He looked down toward his ranch again. "Want to drive down and see the barn?"

She suppressed a chuckle. Was he shy about giving her a tour of the house unchaperoned? His steady blue eyes were watching her, waiting for her answer. "What's in the barn?"

"Well, two box stalls, among other things."

"Two?"

He nodded. "In case you ever want to bring Lancelot over for a visit. Or something."

Her laugh burbled out. His brows shot up again, and she flung her arms around his neck.

"I'd love to see the barn."

"Would you?" he asked softly. He lowered his face toward hers and gently kissed her.

Ruby snuggled into his embrace. When he released her, she sighed. "Yes, I surely would."

epilogue

June twelfth dawned clear and bright. Ruby leaped out of bed and pulled on her jeans. She hurried out to the barn, but her father had beaten her to it and was already measuring out feed for Lancelot.

"You get right back in the house, young lady. You are not going to muck out the barn on your wedding day."

"Oh, Dad! I'll take a shower afterward."

"No way. I'm doing your barn chores this morning, and that's final."

Lancelot poked his head out over the half door of his stall and whickered. She gave her father a quick hug. "Thank you. Just let me say good morning to Lancelot. Then I'll leave you alone."

"You'd better."

She laughed. "I promise." She walked down the barn alley and reached up to scratch the palomino's ears. "I won't be seeing you for a few days. But then we'll come get you and move you over to Chuck's ranch. You and Rascal can race around the pasture together all you want."

Lancelot rubbed his cheek against her arm, and she burrowed her fingers under his white forelock to reach another of his favorite scratching spots.

"You're really going to love the ranch. And you can drink right out of the creek."

"All right, young lady." Her father stood behind her with a lead rope. "Just because you and Chuck won that fancy ride up in Sheridan, you think you can boss the barn help around now. Skedaddle, you hear me?"

Ruby gave Lancelot a last pat and scampered for the barn door. "Okay, Dad, this time you get your way."

She stepped out into the sunshine and inhaled deeply. She would miss the home place, and she would miss Mom and Dad. But she would be only a few miles away, and she had a huge store of memories. This was the right time to step into her new life, with Chuck at her side.

A few hours later she and her mother drove to the church in Ruby's Jeep with her cousin Holly. Dylan, Aunt Ruthie, and Uncle Phil would ride over with Dad.

"Are you sure Grandma and Elsie will make it on time?" Ruby asked her mother. "I thought they'd be here an hour ago."

"Yes," her mother assured her. "When she called, Grandma said they'd had a slight delay, but they'll be at the church in plenty of time." She put on the turn signal for the church driveway.

Holly squealed. "Look, Aunt Linda! There they are."

Ruby looked down the road. Sure enough, there came the hot pink semi with gold lettering across the hood: "Groovy Grannies."

She leaped out of the Jeep and waited in the parking lot while Elsie expertly parked the big truck at the far side of the pavement out of the way. The jake brake gave its familiar rattle, and the passenger door popped open. Grandma climbed down from the passenger side in a stylish powder-blue pants suit. Her silver-white hair was perfectly coiffed. Ruby ran to embrace her.

"Grandma, you look spectacular."

"Well, so do you, dear, though I hope you're not going down the aisle in those dungarees. Now I wanted to tell you,

Elsie and I took care of everything for the wagon ride. After you and Chuck have your week in St. Louis, you can go right to the Moose Valley guest ranch. We've outfitted your covered wagon for you. Here's the reservation." She slipped a folded sheet of paper into Ruby's hand.

"Oh, thank you, Grandma." Ruby gave her another hug.

Elsie, looking as pert as Margaret in a lime-green outfit, came to stand beside her sister-in-law. "It was so much fun setting up the trip for you. I know you and your young man will have a wonderful week on the trail."

"Oh, you two are the best." Ruby gave Elsie a squeeze. "Chuck and I are looking forward to it."

"But hadn't you ought to be putting on your bridal gown?" Grandma asked.

"Yes, hurry, Ruby," her mother said. "You can visit after. Other people are arriving already."

Ruby scooted with Holly, her maid of honor, into the church and to the room set aside for the women to dress in.

"Just in time." Holly closed the door behind them. "I saw a black pickup pulling in right when we reached the church door. I'm pretty sure it was your sweetie and his doll of a brother."

Ruby eyed her in surprise. "You only saw Chuck's brother once."

"Yeah, but he's cute. I can dream, can't I?"

"Well, sure." Ruby reflected she now had an entire new family to enjoy, and Chuck's mom and siblings would be a big part of her life.

"Besides, I'm the one who gets to walk down the aisle with him," Holly added, pulling her dress off the padded hanger.

"True."

Holly gave her a knowing smile. "Of course it's Chuck's

friend I'm really interested in."

"Which one?" Ruby asked absently while unzipping the back of her lace gown.

"Jeff. The horse trainer."

"Oh, that one." Ruby smiled. "He's a great guy."

A soft tap sounded on the door, and the other two brides-maids entered.

"Hey, you're already dressed!" Ruby looked at her two friends and their rose-colored gowns with approval. "What do you know? I picked a color that looks fabulous on all of you."

As they hastened to help Ruby prepare to don her wedding gown, Ruby's mother and grandmother peeked in.

"Hi, Mom," Ruby said. "I'm just about to put this on. Maybe you can help with my veil."

Holly held the dress while Ruby stepped into it and lifted it. Then Ruby turned, and her cousin zipped it for her. When she turned to face the others, her mother's eyes glistened with tears.

"You look so beautiful."

Ruby hugged her. "Thank you."

"I always thought Julie would be with us on this day," her mother whispered.

"I know," Ruby said.

Grandma patted Mom's shoulder. "There now, honey. Julie *is* with us in a way. I'm sure she knows how happy we all are today."

❧

Chuck left the study with the pastor, his brother, Jeff Tavish, and Dr. Hogan. As they entered the sanctuary, his best man and two groomsmen seemed at ease, but Chuck's stomach churned. Amazing that Ruby had agreed to be his wife. The realization delighted him; yet he felt more nervous than he had the day the drug dealers forced him and Ruby to help them recover their contraband.

He stood with his hands folded in the spot the pastor had assigned to him, trying to breathe evenly while his blood rocketed through his veins.

"You okay?" his brother asked softly.

"Yeah. Piece of cake."

"Ha!"

Chuck smiled then, but only for an instant. The organ music changed, and Ruby's friends glided down the aisle toward them. Their rose-colored dresses floated about them. All the girls looked unnatural. Their usually laughing faces regarded him soberly. Makeup perfect, hair pinned up in formal arrangements. They reached their marks at the front of the church and faced the congregation.

Again the music changed, and suddenly everyone stood. Chuck gulped and looked toward the door.

Ruby's smile beamed to him the length of the auditorium. Her brown eyes radiated joy, desire, and satisfaction. Chuck inhaled deeply. He would never regret this day.

He shifted his gaze to Martin's face. How hard would it be for him to hand over his only daughter? Instead of the pain and hesitation Chuck expected to see in his expression, he saw only contentment on his soon-to-be father-in-law's face.

Relieved, he let his gaze rove back to Ruby. Her smile became a grin, and he couldn't help but answer her silently as the music swelled. A few moments later she stood beside him where she belonged.

"Join hands," the minister instructed him.

Chuck reached out, and Ruby slipped her small hands easily into his large ones. He squeezed her fingers and turned with her to face the pastor and begin the rest of life with Ruby.

A Letter To Our Readers

Dear Reader:
In order that we might better contribute to your reading enjoyment, we would appreciate your taking a few minutes to respond to the following questions. We welcome your comments and read each form and letter we receive. When completed, please return to the following:

Fiction Editor
Heartsong Presents
PO Box 719
Uhrichsville, Ohio 44683

1. Did you enjoy reading *Trail to Justice* by Susan Page Davis?
   ❏ Very much! I would like to see more books by this author!
   ❏ Moderately. I would have enjoyed it more if

   _____

   _____

   _____

2. Are you a member of **Heartsong Presents**? ❏ Yes ❏ No
   If no, where did you purchase this book? _____

   _____

3. How would you rate, on a scale from 1 (poor) to 5 (superior), the cover design? _____

4. On a scale from 1 (poor) to 10 (superior), please rate the following elements.

   ____ Heroine   ____ Plot
   ____ Hero   ____ Inspirational theme
   ____ Setting   ____ Secondary characters

5. These characters were special because? _____

_____

_____

6. How has this book inspired your life? _____

_____

_____

7. What settings would you like to see covered in future
   Heartsong Presents books? _____

_____

_____

8. What are some inspirational themes you would like to see
   treated in future books? _____

_____

_____

9. Would you be interested in reading other **Heartsong
   Presents** titles? ❏ Yes ❏ No

10. Please check your age range:
   ❏ Under 18   ❏ 18-24
   ❏ 25-34   ❏ 35-45
   ❏ 46-55   ❏ Over 55

Name _____

Occupation _____

Address _____

City, State, Zip _____

THE RELUCTANT COWGIRL

Welcome to Arkansas where aspiring stage actress Crystal McCord meets up with a handsome yet wary rancher. Is there a future for the dreamer and the cattleman?

Contemporary, paperback, 288 pages, 5³⁄₁₆" x 8"

_____

Heart♥ng

HEARTSONG PRESENTS TITLES AVAILABLE NOW:

— Presents —

Great Inspirational Romance at a Great Price!

Heartsong Presents books are inspirational romances in contemporary and historical settings, designed to give you an enjoyable, spirit-lifting reading experience. You can choose wonderfully written titles from some of today's best authors like Wanda E. Brunstetter, Mary Connealy, Susan Page Davis, Cathy Marie Hake, Joyce Livingston, and many others.

When ordering quantities less than twelve, above titles are $2.97 each.
Not all titles may be available at time of order.

♥

HEARTSONG
PRESENTS

If you love Christian romance...

$10.99

You'll love Heartsong Presents' inspiring and faith-filled romances by today's very best Christian authors...Wanda E. Brunstetter, Mary Connealy, Susan Page Davis, Cathy Marie Hake, and Joyce Livingston, to mention a few!

When you join Heartsong Presents, you'll enjoy four brand-new, mass-market, 176-page books—two contemporary and two historical—that will build you up in your faith when you discover God's role in every relationship you read about!

Imagine...four new romances every four weeks—with men and women like you who long to meet the one God has chosen as the love of their lives...all for the low price of $10.99 postpaid.

Mass Market 176 Pages

To join, simply visit www.heartsong presents.com or complete the coupon below and mail it to the address provided.

✂ -

YES! Sign me up for Hearts♥ng!

NEW MEMBERSHIPS WILL BE SHIPPED IMMEDIATELY!
Send no money now. We'll bill you only $10.99 postpaid with your first shipment of four books. Or for faster action, call 1-740-922-7280.

NAME _____

ADDRESS_____

CITY_____ STATE _____ ZIP _____

MAIL TO: HEARTSONG PRESENTS, P.O. Box 721, Uhrichsville, Ohio 44683
or sign up at WWW.HEARTSONGPRESENTS.COM